LOVE STRIKES TWICE

On a journey to the Scottish harbour town where her grandmother, Cathy, had a love affair that ended in heartbreak many years before, Sarah Barnes can't help but think of how far away her days of strap-hanging on the London Tube seem to be. Currently between jobs, she takes one at a local café — and finds herself falling in love with GP Rory McLean. But when Rory turns out to be the grandson of the man Cathy fell in love with, there are rough waters ahead . . .

JILL BARRY

LOVES STRIKES TWICE

Complete and Unabridged

LINFORD
Leicester

First published in Great Britain in 2018

First Linford Edition
published 2019

*A catalogue record for this book is available
from the British Library.*

ISBN 978–1–4448–4031–5

Published by
F. A. Thorpe (Publishing)
Anstey, Leicestershire

Set by Words & Graphics Ltd.
Anstey, Leicestershire
Printed and bound in Great Britain by
T. J. International Ltd., Padstow, Cornwall

This book is printed on acid-free paper

1

Brief Encounter

'It was a long time ago, Gran. You really don't have to tell me any more,' Sarah said softly.

'Oh, I think I do.' Cathy frowned. 'The place holds so many memories for me . . . I daren't risk someone saying things that might worry you.'

'Maybe I shouldn't go?'

'Nonsense! You've decided to visit friends from uni, and if you're off to Glasgow you might as well go on to Kirlaig.'

'For what it's worth, Gran, I can't believe you'd have done anything wrong, even if you were young and away from home for the first time.'

Cathy stared out at her windswept garden. A scatter of petals from early roses fell like confetti on the lawn.

'I probably broke two hearts,' she said. 'I certainly got my own broken. Believe me, Sarah, my only crime was to fall for someone I shouldn't have.'

'I take it you don't mean Gramps.' Sarah had never heard any of this before.

'I didn't meet your grandfather until two years later. He helped me forget the past and stop blaming myself for what happened in Kirlaig.'

'Mum never said a word.'

'That's because there was no need to tell your mother. I came back from working in the hotel, then I applied to the Civil Service. Your grandfather and I began as office colleagues, then became friends, until one day a workmate told me I must be either blind or stupid!'

'So Gramps wanted to be more than a good friend?'

Cathy nodded.

'He said he always knew he'd marry me one day, but wasn't sure how long it would take to convince me I'd found my Mr Right.' She smiled. 'He was loving and gentle and he used to tease me, insisting he'd saved me from being left on the shelf, as we used to say back then.'

'I'm glad I wasn't around then.' Sarah hesitated. 'I hate to ask this, but do you know whether the man you met all those years ago is still around?'

'I haven't a clue! And before you tell me you can search online, I truly don't want to know. The love we shared remained a secret, but we couldn't go on as we were, so on my next day off I took the train to the nearest big town, where we met for lunch. We were taking a risk meeting in public, so we daren't even hold hands across the table.'

She hesitated.

'His wife was such a lovely person. Elizabeth took a shine to me from the first and I liked and admired her. She used the hotel for meetings of the charity committee she served on, and I used to do some typing for her and go to the house for tea sometimes between my shifts.'

'Poor Gran. I can only imagine how tough things must have been.'

'It was a strain for James, too. My job was only for the summer and I longed for September to arrive as much as I dreaded it.' Cathy shook her head. 'I can't even remember what I ate for lunch that day we met. But I can still see the look on his face when I told him I was going home.'

Her face softened.

'He was such an honourable man. I knew the whole thing was tearing him apart. His wife had found me a live-in job working as a secretary to a laird's wife on a nearby estate, thinking she was doing me a favour as I loved the area so much. How could I possibly have betrayed her trust? I couldn't bear to think of James becoming the subject of gossip and I knew we'd only prolong the agony if I stayed. They were starting a family, for goodness' sake!'

Sarah patted her grandma's hand.

'So his wife never discovered how you felt about each other? You say you kept things secret. Did anyone see you the day you and he met for lunch?'

Cathy hesitated.

'I hope and pray Lizzie never found out, although the minister of the local church happened to be attending a conference in the hotel and I know he noticed us. James went to talk to him after he settled our bill and I've no idea what excuse he gave for being there with me. I can't imagine the minister gossiping, but during my remaining weeks, I'd sometimes go into the stillroom to make a hot drink, and get the feeling I might have been the topic of conversation before I walked in.'

'That must have been awkward.'

'I never got that from Morag, though. She was a good friend and the only person I confided in. She was never judgmental, but I know she worried about scandal.' Cathy stared into the distance. 'You can imagine the disgrace, can't you? The local GP, a respectable married man, making eyes at the English girl who had come to work in a local hotel.'

'It was a long time ago, Gran.'

'I know, but if you do find Morag, please ask her whether the doctor's wife ever found out why I left so abruptly when she'd been so kind to me. If she did, then it's high time I apologised.'

★   ★   ★

Sarah's former room mate, a friend since university, dropped her off at Glasgow Central Station a little closer to departure time than she'd have preferred.

Sarah hurtled on to the platform, shoulder bag swinging and her hair escaping from its ponytail, just in time to make the Fort Robert train. She hefted her case on board, pulled a face at the mountain of luggage already stowed and headed for her seat. Unfortunately there was already some-one sitting there.

'I'm sorry.' She felt in her pocket for her ticket reservation, 'I believe this is my seat.'

The passenger looked up.

'You've reserved seat twenty-seven?'

'Um, yes.'

'Coach B?'

Sarah fixed him with a glare.

'Yes, that's right.'

He looked around.

'I can only assume your reservation slip must have fallen off.' He flipped the lid of his laptop closed. 'My apologies. I'll move.'

Sarah waved her hand at the empty place opposite.

'What if I sit there? There's no reservation on that seat, either. You might as well stay where you are.'

'It would hardly be the gentlemanly thing to do.' For the first time he cracked a smile. 'You must have the seat you booked, but first I'll stow your case.'

He commandeered it and whisked it down the aisle, lifting it on to the pile of luggage — something she'd never have managed to do.

Sarah was still settling herself when the man slid into the opposite place.

'Thank you. That's very kind.'

'My pleasure. I'll try not to encroach upon your space.'

With that, he returned to whatever he was working on, leaving Sarah blown away by the soft Highland lilt of his voice and the sparkle of his eyes.

She gazed through the window while the train slowly pulled away from the platform, heading past dreary sheds and rows of houses until the Clyde came into view below.

The man opposite kept working and, as the landscape took on its own character, Sarah wondered when he'd take notice of it. Or was it so familiar that he couldn't be bothered?

2

Dream On!

An hour into the journey, the trolley attendant reached their table and Sarah's silent travelling companion waited while she gave her order, then closed down his laptop and also requested a coffee and a sandwich. He showed no sign of wanting to chat so she continued to enjoy glimpses of steeply banked lochs and glens as the train progressed.

She had finished a 12-month job contract and needed something else, but gazing at the fascinating backdrop, her days of strap-hanging on the tube and dodging around London's crowded pavements seemed a world away.

Now and then she sneaked a peek at the man opposite. Eventually he put his laptop away and settled back into his seat. But although he gazed at the passing scenery, his expression didn't reflect its serenity.

When the train began slowing for the penultimate stop, Sarah noticed him gathering his belongings before getting to his feet.

'Thanks again for helping with my case,' she said.

'No problem. I'll make sure it's still there before I get off.' His eyes crinkled and a smile lit up his face.

'Don't even joke about it!'

'Ach, it'll be fine. Enjoy your holiday.' And he was gone.

The train stopped and Sarah saw the nearest door swing open. The man jumped on to the platform, handling a large case, satchel and laptop as if they were filled with feathers. He slammed the door shut and raised a hand towards someone further down the platform, making Sarah wonder if his girlfriend or wife was meeting him.

He began trundling his case, passing her window and giving her a nod just as a thunderbolt in the shape of a small boy hurtled towards him. But the child, probably spotting his dad or mum somewhere behind him, had lost all sense of timing.

The man, forced to swerve to avoid the child, caught Sarah's eye and his face split into a rueful grin as if he felt a bit of a fool.

That was when it happened. She hadn't ever before experienced such a powerful sensation, but there was no denying the telltale tummy lurch and the suspicion that her heart was trying to escape her ribcage.

She shook her head. She didn't want to fall in love with someone unattainable only to have history repeat itself. Sarah forced herself to use her common sense.

This was nothing like Grandma Cathy's experience. She was hardly likely to see this man again, was she? Had he been continuing to Kirlaig, she might possibly have got to chat with him, but that wasn't the case. Besides, he'd had ample time to begin a conversation if he had wanted to.

Better to enjoy the glorious sunset, streaks of orange, crimson and flame swirling across the sky as her watch showed her it was almost nine-thirty. Soon she'd be in the car the hotel was sending to meet her. Soon she'd be snuggling down in a comfortable bed.

*   *   *

After arriving the night before, late and too tired to explore, Sarah awoke early, eager to start her search. Surely it couldn't be too difficult to seek out her grandma's old friend?

She'd mentioned the name Morag McGillivray to the driver who collected her at the station, but he was a temporary employee who hadn't yet got to know people in the harbour town. Of course, she could try quizzing one or two of the staff at breakfast, despite not having a clue whether her grandma's old friend had changed her name since the pair were employed at the hotel. Morag, born and brought up in a nearby village, had held the head waitress position while Cathy was one of two receptionists.

Sarah decided to stroll down the hill leading to the quayside. The car ferry was at its mooring, and while the idea of an early morning sail was tempting, her appetite for breakfast was too urgent to ignore.

She made her way back up the road to the hotel, on the way noticing a café, its sign displaying a fat white teapot on a dark red background. This looked a promising place to stop for a morning coffee or a snack lunch.

'Good morning.'

Sarah turned her head and saw a dark-haired man wearing a smart grey suit smiling at her from across the way. She responded, wondering why he was heading towards her.

'You're an early bird, Miss Barnes. I noticed you cross the foyer this morning,' he said.

She hesitated, hoping she hadn't attracted a stalker.

'I'm Alistair Murray, manager of Burns Lodge Hotel. I was off duty last night when you arrived, but I trust you found your room satisfactory?'

Sarah smiled.

'Excellent, thanks. And your driver was waiting on the platform to help me with my luggage when my train arrived.'

'We aim to please. So, are you walking back for breakfast just now?'

'I am, Mr Murray. But please don't let me delay you.'

'I'm going your way. While you're with us, I hope you'll manage to fit in some boat trips. Watch the seals and all that. Are you, em, travelling alone?'

Sarah suppressed a grin. It was none of his business, but he seemed friendly enough, and who could be grumpy on a morning like this?

'I'm following in my grandmother's footsteps.' She groaned. 'I don't mean the children's game. My grandma worked in your hotel many years ago, as a receptionist.'

'Really?' They fell into step, strolling up the incline. 'Does she still live in this area?'

'No, she lives just outside London, not far from my parents and me. She'd probably be amazed to see how this place has changed. I offered to show her some photos online but she said she preferred to remember Kirlaig as it was.'

'The quayside's pretty much the same, according to some of the old boys who come into the hotel for their Sunday lunchtime tipple,' Alistair commented.

'I remember Gran telling me that was the time some of the fishermen would come into the cocktail bar.' Sarah chuckled. 'She had to take her turn serving drinks and she found it hard to figure out their accent. They probably delighted in watching her trying to work out what they were ordering, but she said they were nice to her and she got used to them in the end.'

'She'd find most of the shops have all undergone changes, plus they've increased in number. There probably wasn't as much housing back in those days, either,' Alistair told her. 'So, you're saying your grandma has never returned for a holiday?'

'Never. I think she feels uncertain about returning somewhere she'd find very different from how she remembered it, so it's down to me to make the pilgrimage, so to speak.'

Alistair Murray glanced at his watch.

'Well, I hope you enjoy your stay. I have to get in the car now and collect an American couple arriving off the next ferry.'

Sarah felt puzzled. Surely he could have driven his car down in the first place?

He must have read her mind.

'If I don't do a little walking every day when the opportunity presents itself, my waistline reminds me. The hotel's renowned for its food, so you've been warned, Miss Barnes.'

'I've read some of your menus on the website. And please call me Sarah.'

'Thank you. And maybe you'll return the favour and call me Alistair. Enjoy your breakfast, Sarah.'

He strode up the hill ahead of her.

It was unlikely he'd know an elderly lady who surely must be retired by now, but if she reached a dead end regarding Morag, she'd certainly ask the manager if he had any suggestions. There might not be anyone around who remembered Cathy, but if Morag hadn't moved away, surely someone must know her whereabouts.

★   ★   ★

After breakfast, Sarah decided to ride the car ferry to a nearby island, just to get the feel of being on the water. She was on deck early, watching a small stream of vehicles driving on board and, once the vessel got under way, she walked to the other side of the deck

17

where she perched on a seat, gazing out at sea and sky.

This was so relaxing, and she thought how her grandma would have crossed this stretch of water on several occasions, though she knew Cathy also used her one free day every week to sightsee or visit the cinema in Fort Robert. Sarah intended to see more of Arransay another day if possible.

A movement to her right took her attention. Was that really him? This was a coincidence she hadn't anticipated.

As she hadn't noticed her companion from the train boarding with the rest of the foot passengers, he must have driven on. Now he was leaning on the rail, apparently lost in thought, or maybe, like her, soaking up the peace and enjoying the sea in friendly mood. But should she speak?

When he had glanced at her from the platform the evening before, she'd noticed the warmth in his expression and he seemed friendlier than he had during their journey. But was that

18

because he felt safer, knowing she was unlikely to stroll into his path again?

Exactly as she'd felt drawn to the man when he was so engrossed in his work the evening before, she couldn't resist looking at him now. She wasn't as close this time, but that didn't prevent that tingle in her spine.

He was tall and athletic in build. She could imagine him excelling at sport, perhaps captaining his university football or cricket team. Except his hands put paid to that scenario. They were strong, with long fingers, and nails so well groomed she felt the urge to check her own in case her nail polish was chipped.

He wore no wedding ring, and today the breeze was ruffling his hair and making him look so like a romantic hero that . . .

Stop gawping, Sarah, she told herself firmly.

For one wild moment, she considered approaching him. How would he react?

If he happened to be driving to the island's capital, maybe he'd offer her a lift. Could she resist? No-one cared what she did or where she went. She was on holiday. Finding Morag in Kirlaig could wait till another day.

Sarah's pulse refused to calm down. Was this how her grandma had reacted all those years ago when she'd first set eyes on James the doctor?

3

Only a Heartbeat Away

Rory McLean gripped the ferry's rail hard and stared at the island shimmering in the distance. His mind was focused upon his girlfriend Fiona, staying at her parents' holiday cottage on Arransay. Yet through some mischievous trick of fate, across the deck was the girl he'd travelled with the evening before, and who he'd barely been able to look at because she was quite the most stunning young woman he'd ever seen.

She wasn't conventionally beautiful — that mouth was a tad too generous. But she lit up the railway carriage in a way that stole his breath and, if he hadn't kept a strict hold on what little common sense he still retained, he'd have made an idiot of himself and probably caused his attractive fellow-passenger to sit anywhere else but near him.

To make matters worse, he'd acted like an awkward teenager over that near miss with the boy on the platform, locking gazes with the girl and wishing he'd struck up a conversation earlier.

But how could he move on when he and Fiona were still an item? He hadn't seen her since she'd flown out to Boston to spend Christmas and New Year with him while he and a similarly qualified American doctor were in the second half of a year's job exchange scheme.

He'd enjoyed her company. They'd drunk hot chocolate and mulled wine. Gone ice-skating. Slipped into a church to sing carols on Christmas Eve. Done touristy things and spent cosy evenings snuggled up in his apartment, after going out to dinner or cooking supper together.

Fiona was lovely. He'd known her for ever. His younger sister had told him little Fiona Cameron had a crush on him when he was only sixteen and still prone to blushing. Not a good look when you had hair the colour of his.

Perhaps this close friendship between him and Fiona and their families prevented him from asking her to marry him. Yet, a doctor returning to his roots to begin his career in general practice needed a wife, didn't he? He'd been aware she anticipated some sort of declaration while she stayed with him.

Fiona wasn't a modern kind of young woman and she'd wait for him to seize the initiative. Now, with him taking over the family practice from his father and Fiona still teaching at Kirlaig primary school, the stage was set for their engagement. So why hadn't he sent her flowers? All he had to give her was a bottle of her favourite scent. At least he'd made a note of its name after he'd admired its fragrance while she was staying with him. But a last-minute purchase at the duty-free shop?

The truth was, he still couldn't

propose marriage to Fiona. She deserved someone better. She deserved a husband who was totally and utterly in love with her — not some dim-witted man unable to commit because he was afraid of making an awful mistake.

The train girl was on her feet now, standing at the boat's rail, the breeze whipping her hair around her face. He'd done something that medical science couldn't possibly acknowledge or explain. He'd fallen in love at first sight with a stranger.

And now that stranger was a mere heartbeat away. Rory prayed for guidance.

Deep down, he already knew the answer. He needed to tell Fiona he wasn't the right man for her. He needed to tell her there could be no happy ever after.

He shoved his hands in the pockets of his jacket, making fists so his fingernails dug into his palms. Did he have enough courage to walk over and speak to the girl from the train? And if he did, and was met with a rebuff, would he ignore his uncertainty about a future with Fiona and do the sensible thing after all? Rory knew that was impossible. So what did he have to lose?

Deep in thought, Sarah jumped as the tall man arrived at her side.

'I'm sorry if I startled you. It seemed such a coincidence, seeing you again, I thought I'd better say hello.' He held out his hand. 'The name's Rory. So, are you here on holiday or on business?'

The power of speech seemed to have deserted Sarah. She hadn't expected a friendly greeting, let alone a high voltage smile, displaying even white teeth. And he was waiting for her to respond. She didn't know whether to feel relieved or sorry for herself when he recognised her dilemma.

'I . . . I don't make a habit of accosting young women. If it's of any reassurance to you, I'm a doctor and I live locally.'

She recovered her wits just as he was

about to back away.

'It's all right, I just didn't expect to see you again, that's all. I'm on holiday, staying at the Burns Lodge in Kirlaig.' Whoops, how about that for too much information?

He nodded.

'A good choice. It changed hands a few years back and the hotel group have done an excellent job of refurbishing the old place.' He glanced over his shoulder. 'The crew are preparing for arrival and I'll need to get to my car. I'm afraid I can't offer you a lift as I have some, erm, business to attend to, but I thought it seemed churlish not to speak.'

'I'm staying on board. I wanted to experience the sea trip so I can tell my grandmother I've at least been close to Arransay.'

'You don't want to take the bus? Take a look at the capital?'

He looked puzzled and no wonder.

'I have a project on my mind and I think I should start working on what I wanted to achieve by coming to Kirlaig,' she explained vaguely. 'It might all come to nothing, but the sooner I satisfy my curiosity, the better it'll be.'

'You're from the London area? I spent years studying there.'

'I was born in Surrey.'

'Well, good luck with your quest. If it's anything you think I can help with, you can always give me a ring.' He reached for his wallet and took out a white business card. 'My contact details, just in case. It was good to have met you again.' He began walking away.

'And you.' She remembered she hadn't even told him her name. 'I'm Sarah, by the way,' she called.

He turned his head.

'You suit your name,' he called back.

She almost ran after him, wanting to say she'd changed her mind and could she wait in his car while he dealt with whatever his business was? But common sense prevailed.

He was a doctor, for goodness' sake. And she mustn't appear too eager, even if she was thrilled he'd noticed her and approached, then handed her his card. How weird, though, considering he had barely glanced at her throughout that train journey. Maybe he'd had a lot on his mind.

Rory turned round at the door to the car deck and raised his hand in farewell. One quick nod in her direction and he was through the door and out of view.

The whole episode had lasted for such a short time. But she had his contact details and he wouldn't have handed those over if he never wanted to hear from her again.

Absentmindedly, she stuffed the card into her shoulder bag. What she needed now was a strong cup of coffee down in the ferry's restaurant.

4

Just Good Friends

Rory pulled up outside the white-washed cottage and cut the engine. Now he was here, he wished he didn't have to do what he knew he must. He got out of the car, remembered to reach into the glove compartment for the gift-wrapped bottle of perfume and, without bothering to lock his vehicle, opened the gate and walked up the path towards the front door.

Fiona must have been in the back garden because she appeared dressed in pale blue shorts and white T-shirt. Face to face with her, Rory detected something guarded in her eyes.

'You look well,' she said.

'You, too.' He put his arms around her and hugged her to him, but there was something not quite right. He held her slightly away from him. 'Fiona, there's something I need to say to you.'

No shy smile. No anticipation sparkling in her blue eyes. What was going on here?

He hesitated.

'Is everything all right? Your parents are both well, I hope?'

She nodded.

'Both fit and staying in Edinburgh with my uncle. Look, Rory, I've coffee brewing. Shall we sit outside?'

'That sounds great.'

He waited, gazing into the distance, half-registering sounds of seagulls mewing overhead, until Fiona returned, carrying a tray. He took it from her and she swept a paperback and a pair of striped sunglasses from the tabletop and sat down, setting out cups and saucers alongside a plate of shortbread.

Rory smiled.

'Your mother's special recipe?'

'The very same. Help yourself.'

He picked up his cup, sipped from it then tried to find the right words

— words that somehow still eluded him.

'I, erm, I've brought you a wee gift.' He placed the package beside her saucer.

Fiona put down her cup.

'Thank you very much. But first, I think I should help you out of your predicament.'

His stomach lurched.

'You know already? Fiona, I find it hard to explain myself.'

She reached over and grasped his hand.

'You don't need to. I've done a lot of thinking since I came out to stay with you in Boston. It was obvious we were going nowhere.' She let go of his hand. 'We're fabulous as friends. We're just not destined to be anything other than good mates and you know that as well as I do, so why not stop worrying how you're going to tell me you can't possibly marry me and get stuck into that shortbread!'

Rory could have wept with relief, but

doctors weren't allowed that luxury. He rose and went round the table, putting his arm around Fiona's shoulders and kissing her cheek.

'I never realised you were thinking the same thing. I was obsessed by guilt and regret.'

'Tell me about it!' She wriggled away and rose to face him. 'You're a lovely man and I hope we'll always be friends, but you deserve to be with someone who loves you to distraction and who you know you have to be with, no matter what.'

He nodded.

'I feel the same about you, Fi. I love you, but it's a comfortable kind of love, not the sort that makes the sparks fly, is it?'

She chuckled.

'My schoolgirl crush must have been really annoying for you all those years ago.'

'Not at all. My mates were jealous beyond belief. Still are! Speaking of which, I've not heard from Andy Forbes lately. Now, he definitely had a thing for you.'

He watched her blush.

'Oh, Miss Fiona Cameron, do you have something to tell me?'

'I don't know quite how to say it, considering you and I have just split up.'

'We may not be sailing into the sunset together, but we're still friends.'

She reached across and clutched his hand.

'Andy and me, well, he was back in Kirlaig for his parents' ruby wedding anniversary in April and I got an invitation. He turned up at the party without a plus one, and . . . '

'The rest is history.' Rory's laughter was spontaneous. 'That wee devil. I always knew he had more than a soft spot for my girl!'

'He'd never have tried to come between you and me, please believe that. But we were seated beside each other at the dinner and we ended up dancing together and blethering half the night in front of the log fire. I knew something was happening between us, so, in the end, I asked him out.'

'Was he surprised?'

She sat back.

'I confided my feelings about you and me and how sad it was that we were going to have to part. He'd never have tried to take advantage of you being out of the country.'

'I know that, but thanks for saying it, Fi. I can honestly say I'm delighted for you both, but you tell that wee devil of yours I'm first in line for the job of best man.'

'That wee devil, as you call him, is only an inch shorter than you! As for wedding plans — well, things haven't got that far. Yet.' She busied herself unwrapping her gift.

'You're turning a pretty shade of pink, Fiona. So when do you see your man next? He still works in London, doesn't he?'

'He does. We have lots to think about

regarding our future. I love my job, but . . . '

'It's fine to say it. You love Andy more.'

Fiona nodded.

'Something fearsome, Rory. It's overwhelming but not easy sometimes when we live so far apart.' She chuckled. 'I guess he's stuck with me, though.'

Rory could see the tenderness shining out of her when she talked about the man she loved, but he felt no regrets, only a sense of relief.

'Well, now he has no reason not to propose, and you can tell him from me I said so!'

'Maybe he's waiting for me to pop the question?'

'Well, whichever of you does the asking, I hope he knows he's a lucky son of a gun.'

'We're both lucky. And how about you, Rory? Was there a special girl out in Boston who made the doctor's pulse race? What about the tall blonde nurse who looked like she was sucking a lemon when you took me to that party? Come on, you know you can tell me.'

He held up his hands in mock dismay.

'No way did I ask anyone else out all the time you and I were together. I knew I needed time to think. Time to consider how my decision might affect you as well as me.'

Fiona nodded.

'You're a dear sweet man, Rory McLean. And I hope you meet someone special before too much longer. Now, will you stay for lunch or are you away on the next ferry?'

★   ★   ★

Fearsome. That was how Fiona had described her feelings for Andy. Was that how he'd describe his feelings for Sarah? Had she even told him her surname?

Rory drove back to the ferry departure point, thoughts tumbling round his head as he considered the implications of Fiona's startling pronouncement. But she'd known Andy almost as long as she'd known him. Whereas Sarah was a stranger, about whom he knew nothing, except he liked her voice, her long hair, the direct gaze of those beautiful big eyes, and her composure. Maybe that wasn't such a bad start.

He was hugely relieved about today's outcome. Hadn't he dreaded the moment when he assumed he'd be throwing a thundercloud over Fiona's sunny day? But the darling girl already had everything sorted in her mind and, knowing him as well as she did, understood how he felt, probably better than he did.

But just as Fiona's feelings for Andy were different from the way she felt about Rory, he now understood that when The One walked into your life, you felt struck by lightning, caught like a rabbit in the headlights — all those old cliches rolled into one.

Fearsome love? He was definitely

smitten with Sarah. But how was he supposed to know what to do next?

He'd left her to get in touch, if that was what she wanted. She might be staying in Kirlaig for a few days or a week or two, but certainly no longer.

If he turned up at the hotel, determined to sweep her off her feet, she might sweep him into the garbage can! If he dragged his feet, any precious quality time spent together wouldn't add up to much.

While he was still pondering the best way forward, he'd find himself waving her off from the station and maybe regretting the whole thing ever happened.

As Fiona had reminded him, Kirlaig and London were a long way apart, especially for a busy GP, trying to settle into a job when the person he was replacing was his father, who'd taken over the family practice from his grandfather James. Rory was well aware of the weight of expectation resting upon his shoulders.

But Fiona's parting shot had been wise.

'You'll fall in love one day, Rory. I know you will. And when it happens, don't fight it, but don't ignore it, either. Life's too short to miss out on happiness just because you're afraid to take a chance on love.'

Her words had surprised him. It seemed she'd woken from a kind of trance, and maybe he himself had been partly responsible, simply by inviting her out to Boston where they'd acted like two old friends enjoying their reunion. Which, he supposed, was the perfect description of that time together.

But Andy had better treat Fiona like she was the most precious jewel in the box, or he'd be answering to his old mate Rory and that was a fact.

5

The Search is On

On Deck, Sarah gazed at the busy harbour scene as the ferry drew closer. Rory still occupied her thoughts, but though she longed to see him again, her practical side told her she could well be storing up unhappiness.

He seemed a very together sort of person, probably thirty or so against her twenty-three years. She couldn't help wondering why a professional man, attractive and charming, didn't already have a partner.

Cold fear hit her as she tried to ignore a little voice warning her he might be a big bad wolf. But he was a doctor and . . . and what? Sarah couldn't help but think of what had happened once upon a time in Kirlaig.

She was being fanciful. It was best to

forget him. She needed to concentrate on the matter at hand and leave well alone. Kirlaig hadn't proved lucky for her grandma. But surely fate couldn't play a second cruel trick?

She blinked hard, sucking in her breath while she unzipped her shoulder bag. How could she have been so scatter-brained? With so much on her mind, she'd been stupidly ignorant of Rory's surname. And there it was, staring up at her, bold, black letters on white. Rory McLean — followed by a string of qualifications. The man who'd had such a devastating effect on her wasn't only a high-flyer, but must also be the grandson of Dr James McLean.

At once she could hear her grandma's voice as she spoke that name softly, her eyes suddenly bright with tears, even after all those decades. It had to be the same family.

Sarah had walked right into a trap, except there was no way Rory could be aware of her heritage. She needn't fear a deliberate deception on his part. But if Dr McLean's wife had learned of her husband's clandestine relationship and those whispered rumours gathered momentum, once Rory discovered who Sarah was and why she'd come here all these years later, he might well decide to have nothing more to do with her. But surely no-one need bear a grudge about something that happened so long ago.

As soon as Sarah set foot on the quayside, she headed for the shops. The pharmacy sign wasn't hard to spot and she went inside. If Kirlaig carried on pretending it sat on the Mediterranean coast, she'd be wise to protect her skin.

She chose her preferred brand of sunscreen and approached the counter.

'Just this one, please.' She held out a £10 note to the young assistant whose smile was welcoming.

'You've caught the sun already,' the girl said. 'You need to take care this time of year.'

'The weather's beautiful so I mustn't complain.' Sarah hesitated. 'I wonder if

I could ask you something?'

'Ask away, but the pharmacist's on his break just now.'

'It's not a health issue. I'm hoping to get in touch with a lady called Morag. She'd be in her seventies now, I think. Her name was Morag McGillivray, but she could have married or moved out of the village.'

The assistant frowned.

'I know two people called Morag, but one's my aunt and the other's someone I went to school with. I can ask the pharmacist when he comes back. He'll probably want to know who it is enquiring.'

'I'm Sarah Barnes, but it won't mean anything to anyone.'

'OK. Maybe you could call back later if you haven't had any luck.' She grinned. 'The pharmacist's pretty ancient and he knows everyone around here.'

'Thank you. I'll go and have a snack. The people who run the café may be able to help.'

'That'll be Mrs Lennox and a wee girl called Rhona. Mrs Lennox is old.'

'Cheers,' Sarah said and turned towards the door.

Hopefully Mrs Lennox wouldn't turn out to be a mere forty-something. People older than thirty were geriatrics according to most teenagers.

On arriving at the café, Sarah looked through the window before entering. A few tables were occupied and she made her way to the counter, behind which stood a young girl, her hair covered by a neat cap.

The girl turned away from the coffee machine to greet her.

'I'll be with you in a moment.'

'That's OK.' Sarah's gaze took in the mouth-watering selection of cakes and cookies nestling beneath glass domes.

The sea air must have given her an appetite, despite having eaten such a big breakfast. Chocolate cream gateau, tiffin bursting with plump glacé cherries, chunks of golden shortbread . . .

she was finding it impossible to make a choice.

'Right, then. What can I get you?'

'A cup of filter coffee, please, with a little milk. And a slice of that dark, sticky-looking cake because it looks much too good to miss.'

The girl nodded.

'Our date loaf's a big favourite. If you take a seat, I'll bring your order over.'

Sarah headed for a small table in the far corner. When her snack arrived, she'd ask whether the name Morag meant anything to the girl. It was worth a try, but she'd probably have better luck if she spoke to someone from an older generation.

If only Cathy had kept in touch with her old friend. But it was pointless to wish that, and if she had no luck here, she wouldn't give up. There was always the pharmacist, though didn't they have to be careful over security issues these days? For her part, she certainly didn't intend giving anything away, either.

Sarah took out her phone. There

were no messages.

She had a sudden, overwhelming urge to text Rory. But he was bound to be busy, though she couldn't help wondering why he'd been on the car ferry rather than sitting in his surgery doling out prescriptions.

He'd left the train at the stop before the terminus, so he obviously wasn't living or staying in Kirlaig. Should she contact him or not?

The arrival of her order saved her from deciding.

'Thank you.' Sarah smiled up at her waitress. 'Am I right in thinking you're Rhona?'

'Aye, but how do you know my name?'

'The young lady who works at the pharmacy told me when I said I intended coming here. I'm hoping to trace an old friend of my grandmother's, so I'm asking people whether they know her. I've no idea if the friend, Morag McGillivray that is, has changed her name, so it's not easy.'

'I'll ask Mrs Lennox if she knows.'

'Ask Mrs Lennox if she knows what?'

Sarah turned towards the voice. An older lady, wearing a spotless white apron over a crimson dress, stood in the kitchen doorway. Her grey hair was drawn into a bun beneath the same kind of cap as her helper wore. Her face looked as though it had hosted millions of smiles across the years, but her expression was wary as she sized up her customer.

Sarah rose and walked up to the counter. Now she could see the café owner wore a surgical boot on her left foot and she'd propped a walking stick against the door frame.

'I wonder if you can help,' Sarah said. 'I'm trying to contact my grandmother's old friend, Morag McGillivray.'

'Is that right? Then you're looking at her. Will I come and sit down with you while you enjoy your snack?'

6

Shock Revelation

Rory McLean drove up the hill towards his grandmother's house, feeling as if he'd been walking through treacle, but was now free from the sticky morass and into easier territory.

Who'd have thought his old schoolmate, after carrying a torch for Fiona all this time, would finally make his feelings known?

He must message Andy, sending his best wishes and reassurance that not one scrap of bitterness existed. Surely an engagement must be on the cards now there was no longer that unspoken bond between Fiona and himself? Rory felt a tad wistful and not a little envious of the couple's joy, despite his relief.

Now he must focus on taking over from his father and familiarising himself with routines and the patient list, while Dr Will McLean gradually decreased his workload. The female medic, who was his father's partner in the practice, worked part-time and Rory would be sharing the workload with her.

Surgeries were also held in the next village. It wasn't the best of times for a hard-pressed doctor to be pursuing romance, but Rory felt strongly that if life thrust an opportunity in your path, you should think very carefully before ignoring it.

If Sarah didn't contact him in the next day or two, he'd leave a note at her hotel's reception desk. It would be good to relax over a coffee or a glass of wine, though his father, who held strict views about a doctor's image, especially within a community like this, would frown over the latter. Will McLean enjoyed a dram, but only when at home or visiting friends or family.

Rory glanced at his dashboard clock, noting he was well on time for lunch. He smiled to himself, recalling one time when he was still a medical student and he returned from university for the holidays, and turned up an hour later than invited. Luckily, the homemade leek and potato soup hadn't spoiled, nor had the apple pie, though his grandmother had likened the custard, made in advance, to wallpaper paste.

'It certainly doesn't taste anything but delicious,' Rory had soothed.

'Practising our bedside manner already, are we?' she'd teased.

He steered his station wagon through the gates of Rowan House and pulled up beside the white Mini belonging to Elizabeth McLean's housekeeper, Joan, who came in for a few hours most days.

Rory switched off his engine and ferreted in his satchel for the gift-wrapped silk scarf he'd chosen for his grandma. The third present purchased in the duty free lounge was a silver harp-shaped brooch he thought would suit his mother, although, like Fiona's parents, Sheena McLean was away from home, in her case visiting St

Andrews to research a feature she'd been asked to write for a travel magazine.

Rory's tan leather loafers crunched over the gravelled drive as he approached the front door. His grandma answered the bell quickly, making him wonder if she'd been watching out for him. She was using her walking stick and looked elegant in a soft lilac-coloured wool dress.

'Nana, you look a million dollars.'

'Fiddlesticks, young Rory. I might have known you'd come back spouting a load of flannel, not to mention Americanisms.' She moved aside so he could step inside. 'Will I get a hug? And have you seen that young woman of yours yet?'

'Yes. And yes. I've something to tell you.' He put his arms around Lizzie and hugged her. 'And I've brought you a little something.'

'You shouldn't waste your money,' she scolded, accepting the package. 'But thank you for thinking of me.'

'Well, you've had another birthday

since I've been away, Nana.' He adjusted his stride so they walked towards the sitting room together.

'Don't remind me! Now, I've put a couple of beers in the fridge for you and maybe you'll pour an old lady a sherry?'

'My pleasure, but I don't see any old lady.'

'You get worse!'

'Does that mean I'm allowed to fetch a beer?'

'By all means. You'll find Joan in the kitchen. After we've eaten lunch, she'll wash up then take Archie for a walk.'

'Excellent. So where is the old boy?' Rory walked across to the sideboard while his grandmother settled into her favourite chair.

'At the surgery, of course! Where did you expect him to be? He'll be along for his lunch in a while.'

Rory hid a smile.

'I meant the dog, not Pa. Here you go, Nana.' He handed her a glass of sherry.

His grandmother looked impatient.

'The dog's probably asleep in his bed in the kitchen. Now, will you fetch your drink and come back and tell me what it is you're fretting over? It's obviously not good news.'

★   ★   ★

Sarah felt puzzled.

'You're grandma's friend from the hotel? I don't believe it!'

'What don't you believe? I didn't become Mrs Lennox until I turned forty, but sadly your grandma and I lost contact about ten years after she left Scotland. Something to do with moving house, I reckon.'

'You realise who I am, then?'

Morag smiled.

'Well, there's no mistaking Cathy's eyes and that hair. And I don't think you could be her daughter.'

'I suppose not. But what I find puzzling is how neither the pharmacy assistant nor Rhona suggested the

Morag I mentioned might be you.'

Morag Lennox smiled up at her assistant who was bringing her a cup of tea before scuttling back behind the counter.

'The pharmacy assistant's scared to blow her nose without permission and Rhona's still learning the job. I never reveal personal information to my employees until they've been with me a while. That wee girl knows me only as Mrs Lennox and that's how it should be.'

'My grandma told me you were always a stickler for things being right.' Sarah bit into a chunk of date loaf and chewed thoughtfully.

'What d'you think of it?'

'Paradise on a plate!'

'I wish I could say there was plenty more where that came from, but this pesky foot of mine won't let me do as much as I'd like. It's lovely to meet you, my dear, and I've a heap of questions, but I'm afraid you've caught me at a difficult time.'

'I'm so sorry. How did you get injured?'

Morag snorted.

'Trying to do a bit of DIY and tripping up. I have to wear this contraption for a while longer.'

'Is there no-one you can call upon for help?'

Morag shook her head.

'My sister's moved away, though she came and helped when I was first laid up. My friends all have jobs or would run a mile rather than bake for the café. The wee girl's inexperienced, though I suppose I could talk her through my recipes if only I had someone to wait on the customers.'

'I see.' Sarah sipped her coffee. 'If everything's as delicious as what I'm sampling, I imagine you must get very busy?'

'That's what I aim for. But tell me how your grandma is. I know she married because we were still in touch then.' Morag's expression became thoughtful. 'I hope she found happiness after, after all that . . . '

'She did.' Sarah leaned across the table. 'She's told me what happened while she was living in Kirlaig. It must have been awful for her, but she said meeting my gramps was the best thing that could have happened. She's only been widowed three years so they had a long time together.'

Morag's expression was wistful.

'Believe me, it's never enough time if you're with the right one. But what you say makes me very happy indeed. Yes, it was a difficult situation for Cathy and James McLean. I don't believe either of them would have intended to fall in love. It was as if, once that man set eyes on our new receptionist, he became mesmerised.'

'Mesmerised? Are you saying my grandma enchanted him?'

'Certainly not by intention. She was a quiet lassie, always polite to other staff members as well as guests. But it was the same for her once she set eyes on the doctor. It was as if they were two magnets, pulling towards one another, but always trying to defy the force of gravity. Longing to be together but knowing it couldn't be.'

Morag bit her lip. Sarah reached across and patted her hand.

'I know very little about the situation,' Sarah said. 'I think Grandma was frightened to say too much, what with me coming here and not knowing who might still be around from the old days.'

Morag greeted someone who'd just come in.

'So what actually does bring you here, Sarah?'

Sarah shrugged.

'I had a trip to Glasgow planned to catch up with girlfriends I shared a house with while I was at uni. My parents are taking a long holiday, so I've spent more time than usual with Gran. That's just for a bit of company,' she added. 'She's perfectly capable of coping on her own.'

'That's good to hear,' Morag said. 'I

have a few more years than she has.'

'Anyway, as I'm between jobs, I decided to visit Kirlaig. I did ask my grandma if she preferred I didn't, but she said if I was going to Glasgow, I might as well make the most of it and visit.'

'And Cathy suggested you try to find me?'

'Yes.'

'Any special reason? Not that I'm not delighted.'

'And I'm thrilled to have found you so quickly! I'll give you her address and phone number so you can ring her when you want to. I think she's anxious to put certain things to rest. She fears that after she left at the end of that summer, people may have been speculating about a situation that didn't reflect well on her or upon the, um, doctor.'

Morag compressed her lips before answering.

'There was talk. I shouldn't say more than that.'

Sarah wiped her sticky fingers on a paper napkin. She was determined to get to the bottom of this, no matter how long it took, but her turning up out of the blue must be a shock for her grandma's friend.

'Did Cathy mention the doctor's wife?' Morag asked.

'She did. She told me she got on well with Elizabeth and the two of them became friendly. She said she could have stayed on at the end of the season, because Elizabeth found her a live-in job.'

Morag closed her eyes for a moment.

'Lizzie McLean was — still is — a fine woman. But that situation was a house of cards waiting to tumble around all three of those unfortunate people.'

Sarah held her breath, afraid to ask the question but desperate for the answer.

'Did Mrs McLean ever find out?'

'Find out what had been going on behind her back? We have to face the truth, my girl. There was deception involved and don't you forget it.'

Sarah squirmed, suddenly uncomfortable.

'I'm aware of that, Mrs Lennox.'

'Ah, but it's Morag to you, child.'

'Obviously they shouldn't have admitted their feelings for one another, Morag. Nor can I believe how Grandma's still beating herself up over it after all these years. But I wish I knew whether the doctor's wife ever discovered her husband held feelings for someone she considered a friend.'

'I remember Lizzie feeling hurt when Cathy told her she was going back home. I felt terribly torn — I was losing a friend, too, remember — but Cathy and I went for a long walk one afternoon between shifts and she poured her heart out. She asked me what she should do.'

'No pressure, then,' Sarah murmured.

'Precisely. But your grandma didn't really need advice. She knew what was right and proper.' Morag spoke even more quietly.

'Of course, it turned out there was a bairn on the way by then.'

Sarah almost choked on her last mouthful of coffee.

'No! Oh, please don't say that's what happened to my gran! Why ever didn't she tell me?'

7

A Touch of Magic

'Thanks for telling me about your decision, Rory.'

'It's as much Fiona's decision as mine, Nana.' He sat down again. 'I must say I was relieved to know her feelings matched mine.'

'She's a lovely young woman. Does a great job down at the school, so I'm told.'

Rory decided not to mention Fiona's dilemma regarding her future.

'Fi enjoys teaching. We'll still be friends, the pair of us. Still keep in touch.'

Elizabeth shook her head.

'I find modern ways quite baffling. In my day, we had friends who were girls and, if we were fortunate, one special boyfriend who we'd eventually marry.'

'Well, you fitted that pattern, didn't you?'

'Oh, yes, although that didn't mean our married life was all sunshine and no showers. I have a suspicion you and Fiona might have had a very happy union if the pair of you hadn't taken so long to get round to doing something about it.'

'Oh, come on, Nana. I think we both know there has to be a certain something, a touch of magic maybe, to help make a happy marriage.'

She snorted.

'Magic? That's rich, coming from a scientist!'

'Just because I'm following the family line of doctors doesn't mean I've no romance in my soul.' He sipped at his drink, unable to stop thinking of his train journey. 'I even think there might be such a thing as love at first sight.'

'Do you indeed? And who might the young woman in question be, may I ask?'

Startled, Rory looked at his grandmother.

'I didn't mean — I wasn't referring to myself.'

'Balderdash! I may be ancient but I'm not dotty.' She leaned forward. 'Come on, let me into your secret before your father arrives. I promise not to spill the beans.'

'It's crazy, I know. But there was this girl on the train from Glasgow last night. We didn't get off on the right foot, mainly because I was shocked at the way I reacted. But there was something so different about her . . . '

'In what way?'

Rory folded his arms across his chest.

'Quirky is maybe how I'd describe her.'

'Hmm. Is she English?'

'She is. She's also young and very pretty.'

'So is Fiona.'

'I know, but this girl's different.'

'Did you exchange names? Or did the cat get your tongues, the pair of you?'

'That's the weird thing. I got off at Gairton, of course. Alex was waiting to drive me home.'

'Have you told your sister about you and Fiona?'

He shook his head.

'Not yet, but I will later. Anyway, the English girl was going on to Kirlaig and we hadn't got talking during the journey apart from a wee chat at the start. But she turned up on the ferry to Arransay this morning when I was going to visit Fiona. So I spoke to her.'

'You wanted to chat her up. So you must fancy this lass, then?'

'It's a good job Pa isn't here. He'd be shocked to hear you say such things.'

She chuckled.

'Will doesn't take after his mother, that's for sure. Nothing much shocks me, Rory.'

'I know that, but I don't intend hitting the Kirlaig headlines. I know what this place can be like when it comes to gossip.'

Puzzled, he watched his grandmother

seem to shrink into her chair. Her eyes had lost their sparkle.

She looked down at her hands, the skin wrinkled and papery now, but still adorned with jewelled rings she'd probably worn all of the time he'd known her. He was wondering what he'd said to upset her when the phone on the hall stand began ringing.

'Nana? Shall I get that?'

'Please.' Still she didn't look at him.

In the hallway, he picked up the receiver and spoke to his father.

'I'll tell Nana you'll be another half hour at most. If she wants to start without you, I'd better follow suit. OK, see you soon.'

Returning to the sitting room, he found Elizabeth sitting up straight, gazing at the china dogs and pretty pillboxes decorating the mantelpiece.

'That was Pa. He'll be here by half past one but we're to start without him if we wish. What do you think?'

'I think I must have received hundreds of similar messages over the years, Rory. Would you tell Joan we'll wait for your father, please?'

Rory did as he was told, then came back and took Elizabeth's glass away for a refill.

'You worried me for a while there,' he said, sitting down again. 'Did I say something to upset you?'

She bit her lip.

'I'm being silly. Sometimes the past comes back to haunt us. There was a time, a long, long while back, when I feared local gossip might wreck my marriage.'

Rory sat up straight.

'Are you serious?'

'Indeed I am.'

'You surprise me. I've never heard a whisper of any trouble between you and Grampy.'

'I'm speaking of the time before the children came along, not long before your father made his appearance in the world. I'd realised there was something wrong between my Jamie and me. He was out a lot in those days, of course.'

'As was my pa,' Rory said. 'I've no illusions as to the kind of life I'm in for.'

'But even when James was home with me, it was as if he were somewhere else. He was still kind and loving, but sometimes I'd catch him unawares. There would be such a troubled expression on his face that I couldn't stop asking him what the matter was. He'd smile and make an excuse about figuring out a patient's treatment or some such thing, but I wasn't fooled.'

'Not a lot gets past you, Nana.'

'Hmm. I think I must have been very stupid because I never realised he'd fallen for a young woman I'd become friendly with.'

Rory's stomach lurched.

'But that must have been dreadful for you. When . . . how did you find out?'

'I found out when whatever was between Jamie and this girl ended. She left her job and went back to England.'

'Where did she work?'

'At the hotel.'

'The Burns Lodge?'

'It went under another name back then. She was a receptionist for the summer season back then. Your father was born the following spring.'

Rory slowly shook his head.

'I'm so sorry. I never had a clue about any of this. Stop me if this is upsetting for you, but did village gossip reach your ears or did Grampy tell you himself?'

She smiled.

'He did. Jamie was such an honest man. He must have tortured himself half to death with guilt. I felt so sorry for him. He could easily have kept it to himself, but he chose to speak up.'

Rory couldn't bring himself to ask for more details.

'And you forgave him. He was very lucky to have such a loyal wife, but can I ask why you're telling me this now?'

Elizabeth sipped her sherry.

'Because you told me about yourself and Fiona so I wouldn't have to find out from someone else. Because I'm at the far end of my life and I want you to know you don't have to be perfect to make a success of marriage. Being wed means a whole batch of things, tolerance and forgiveness being two of them. You should remember everything and everyone comes with flaws.'

'You think Fiona and I are making a mistake, not giving marriage a try? Believe me, we're not. She's in love with one of my old friends and I'm delighted for the pair of them.'

'That's good, then. Maybe this young English lady is exactly what you need right now.'

'Maybe not. I don't know how long Sarah intends staying in Kirlaig, but I doubt she'll be around long.'

'So she's called Sarah? And what will you do next?'

'Knuckle down to work if Pa has anything to do with it.'

His grandmother hesitated.

'You'll probably wonder why I'm saying this, but what happened with your grandfather and the English girl actually brought him and me closer together. Soon before I found out about them, I discovered I was expecting a happy event. There was no time for hissy fits. No time for blaming. Your father was on the way and Jamie and I were starting a family together.'

'Indeed. Yet you say you were friendly with this girl. How did that work out?'

'I visited the hotel for meetings or the occasional lunch. She was always friendly and helpful and I knew she was far from home so I invited her here on a few occasions. She'd taken a liking to Kirlaig, but the hotel closed after the summer season in those days and I heard about a vacancy for a live-in companion and told her about it. I don't think Cathy was a bad person, and maybe the fact that I was thinking about her, doing her a kindness, made her see sense.'

'Thank goodness for that.'

'There are always two sides, Rory. Jamie admitted to having a crush. Our engagement had been a long one because of his medical training and family matters. He got his chance of a little magic and he took it.' She shrugged. 'Maybe we'd been taking each other for granted. Life moved on and I'm certain we both found much joy in our marriage, especially through our children.'

'I think you're telling me not to sit back and watch other people having fun?'

'I'm telling you that a holiday romance, a summer fling or whatever you like to call it, needn't necessarily be a bad thing. You're a young single man and you'll be an excellent GP. Don't miss out on your own touch of magic.'

Startled, Rory thought of Fiona's words as well. But he could hear a car pulling on to the driveway.

His grandma turned her head.

'There's Will now. We can eat.'

'Elizabeth McLean, you're an amazing lady. I'll let you know how things turn out with Sarah.'

Sarah took a deep breath. Thankfully, Morag had been quick to put her right. The doctor and his wife were on the verge of parenthood around the time Cathy left.

'Are you all right now?' Morag's face was concerned.

'Fine, thanks. I'm sorry about getting the wrong end of the stick.'

'I can't blame you for thinking the worst. But fortunately for all concerned, that particular problem didn't arise. Back then, of course, it would have turned your grandma's life upside-down. It doesn't bear thinking about.'

'I understand. One half of me feels cross that she seems to have lost her head, and the other half can't help feeling sorry for her and the doctor. At least she went on to have a happy marriage, thank goodness.'

'So did James McLean, although he never made old bones. Elizabeth acted with dignity and common sense. It's funny, but her grandson, though I haven't seen him lately, reminds me a lot of her. He's about to take over as GP. His father's not in the best of health and he's needing to shed part of his workload and maybe retire completely after young Rory gets into his stride.'

Sarah stared at her.

'So Rory McLean is Elizabeth McLean's grandson?' She knew the answer already, but that didn't stop her needing to hear it from Morag's own lips.

'He is. There's a granddaughter, too. Alexandra teaches in Edinburgh, but she's home in Gairton just now, though her mother's off somewhere. I can't keep pace with the lot of them, but I know Rory's just got back from America. He'll be a safe pair of hands at the surgery and I wouldn't be surprised to hear news of an engagement soon. His sweetheart teaches at the primary school. Fiona and Alexandra went to the same boarding school and both became teachers so the girls are good friends.'

Sarah swallowed hard.

'That's nice,' she managed to croak.

'Pardon me, but you sounded as though you already knew about Rory,' Morag said.

'Our paths have crossed. We had a brief conversation on the ferry and he gave . . . he told me his name, that's all. I'd forgotten Grandma mentioned the family surname to me, and when I found out Rory's I put two and two together.'

Morag glanced around as the café door opened.

'I'd better go and help Rhona. Will you write down your grandma's contact details for me, please?'

'Of course.' Sarah delved in her bag for paper and pen. 'And I'll be back soon.'

8

It's a Date

Sarah insisted on paying her bill and left the café, her head buzzing. Poor Morag was struggling to cope while Sarah had time on her hands. She wasn't at all surprised to hear Rory McLean had a girlfriend. But she was surprised that he'd so readily given his card to a young, single woman who surely didn't appear to be in imminent need of medical advice.

She must have read more into his gesture than he'd intended, but thank goodness Morag explained the situation. It would have been horrendously embarrassing if she'd rung Rory to see if he fancied meeting up for a drink and his girlfriend happened to be there when his phone rang. She couldn't help thinking it would have served him right

— but what a foolish man.

More and more, Sarah was convincing herself James McLean must have been very misguided to embark upon a flirtation with a receptionist from the local hotel. At least Cathy had left for home before the tongues really did start wagging.

Sarah felt a little guilty, condemning the late doctor, but now she knew his grandson had a girlfriend, Sarah felt indignant on Cathy's behalf, as well as her own. All she hoped now was that she managed to avoid any further meetings with the latest in the line of McLean medical men.

Sarah continued walking up the hill, passing the hotel and heading around and behind it, tackling the grassy slope until, out of breath, she sank down on a heathery outcrop and stared at the harbour below.

Slowly her turmoil of thoughts began to settle into the right places. Maybe it was something to do with the peace and quiet — watching the serene sea basking on a sunny afternoon while boats came and went. Or maybe it was the way Morag had provided such an honest account of a relationship that could so easily have spilled into a dark and upsetting situation.

To Sarah, it sounded as though her grandma had been the stronger one of the unfortunate couple risking disapproval and worse. Elizabeth McLean should be made aware of this. She longed to visit the doctor's widow and convince her how much guilt Cathy still bore. She'd hated seeing her grandma so forlorn when recalling the events of decades before. Shouldn't her granddaughter try to spell out the truth?

As for Rory, the only way Sarah could deal with him was to ignore him. That meant stopping him from making those unexpected appearances in her mind's eye — but that was easier said than done.

She sighed. Had he even the least idea of what his grandfather and her grandmother had put themselves through back then? If he was aware of the story only from Lizzie McLean's viewpoint, he, too, should be made aware of Cathy's predicament and . . . yes, her strength of character.

If he knew nothing, it was probably best to leave things that way. As he was clearly out of bounds for Sarah, at least she was spared the embarrassment of him rejecting her as a possible holiday romance.

What she really wanted to do was offer assistance to Morag for at least a few days, so the café could continue running efficiently. That would be a little thank-you to the café owner for the support and friendship she'd given to Cathy, even if the two women had lost contact over the years. Morag was something of a closed book, obviously widowed, but seemingly with no family or friends prepared to help her over a tricky time.

Sarah got to her feet and brushed down her jeans. It wouldn't hurt to offer her services. But first she'd go back to the hotel and write her grandmother a letter. She'd include a postcard showing the modernised version of the hotel where Cathy used to work, and reassure her she'd spent time with Morag and that her old friend was delighted to be put in touch with her again.

When she walked through the hotel's swing doors, she saw the manager crossing the foyer. He noticed her at once.

'May I help with anything, Sarah? Or are you just passing through?'

'I'm fine, thanks, Alistair.' She hesitated. 'Come to think of it, I could do with a sheet of notepaper and an envelope if that's not too much trouble. I'd like to buy a postcard, too.'

He nodded.

'I'll let you have those, plus a card with our compliments. But why aren't you still out and about on such a beautiful afternoon, if that's not too impertinent a question?'

She followed him over to the desk.

'I need to get some thoughts down

on paper before I do anything else. Maybe I'll go out again later.'

He handed her the stationery.

'I'm glad I saw you. As it happens I have a free evening.' He straightened his tie. 'I've, um, I've been wondering if you might fancy driving a few miles along the coast to a seafood restaurant I enjoy visiting now and then?'

He was looking anxiously at her. He seemed a pleasant enough man, but she wanted to know where she stood, regardless of whether she decided to ring Rory McLean and request a non-medical appointment so she could give him a piece of her mind.

'Do you make a habit of asking your guests out to dinner?'

Alistair chuckled.

'Fair point. No, I do not. Mainly because I work antisocial hours, but to be honest, we don't get that many single young women staying with us.'

She shook her head.

'I hope you're not feeling sorry for me, Mr Murray.'

'I don't feel in the least sorry for you, Miss Barnes.' His glance was admiring. 'I understand you may already have plans, but I'd very much appreciate your company.'

He must have noticed her glancing at his left hand.

'I'm not married, nor even engaged. As they say, I'm currently single.'

'Me, too. All right, then, I'd love to come out with you.'

'Right, I'll see you at seven o'clock. I'll be waiting in the car park with my trusty steed.'

Smiling, she headed up the stairs to her room. She hadn't come to Kirlaig in search of male company, but for some reason it seemed to be finding her. And it would be interesting to know whether the hotel manager knew any of the McLean family history.

★   ★   ★

Rory excused himself and left his grandmother and his father drinking coffee in the sitting room. He needed to go home and finish unpacking, and also to catch up with a thousand other things demanding his attention.

He wasn't officially due to begin his new role until the beginning of next month, but he was happy to hold surgery now and then to get his feet beneath the table, as his father had declared over lunch.

He was finding it difficult to put Sarah out of his mind. Much as he realised there was little point in hankering after someone who was only visiting and who lived probably 500 miles away from him, he longed to see her again.

He helped himself to a sheet of notepaper from his grandmother's bureau and sat down in the empty dining room to write a note.

'Dear Sarah, It was good to see you again on the ferry and I hope you enjoyed your day. How does meeting up for a drink and a meal sound? Life will get a whole lot busier for me soon and I imagine you'll be off back to London once your holiday ends. Rather than ring the hotel, I'm delivering this note by hand. You know how to get in touch and if you can bear the thought of spending time with me, I shall look forward to your phone call so we can make arrangements. Rory McLean.'

He sealed the envelope and let himself out via the front door. Not too many minutes later he parked on the forecourt of the Burns Lodge. Inside the foyer, a dark-haired man looked enquiringly at him as Rory approached the desk.

'Good afternoon, sir. How may I help you?'

Rory noticed the man's name badge, identifying him as manager. He smiled and took the letter from his pocket.

'I'd be obliged if you could see this reaches a guest who's staying here.'

He noticed Alistair's surprised expression as he read the name on the envelope.

'I'll personally ensure Miss Barnes

receives your letter, sir. Is there anything else I can help you with?'

'There's nothing else, thanks.' Rory glanced around him. 'I haven't been here for a while. You keep a tidy hotel, by the looks of things.'

Alistair inclined his head.

'I have an excellent team, sir. Thank you for your compliment. Might I ask whether you live locally?'

'I've only just returned from a year in the States, but my family's been around these parts for a very long time.'

'Would you be Will McLean's son, by any chance?'

Rory grinned.

'I'm Rory McLean, yes. How did you know? As if I couldn't guess!'

Alistair nodded.

'The local grapevine has it you're about to take over from your father. I wish you all the best. I've only been in my post for six months, but even I know he'll be a hard act to follow.'

'I'm well aware of that fact, Mr Murray. Thanks for your good wishes.'

Rory turned and headed for the entrance.

The manager had sounded as though he was speaking through gritted teeth and, for the life of him, Rory couldn't understand why.

9

A Problem Shared . . .

Sarah chose a pale pink dress patterned with seahorses and shells. She didn't want to look too glamorous, so used the minimum of make-up and her usual light floral perfume. She wore strappy green sandals and carried a matching handbag.

Ignoring the lift, she walked downstairs and glanced at the reception desk on her way to the car park exit.

'Miss Barnes? There's a message for you.' The woman on duty held out a white envelope as Sarah approached. 'There you go. It's been hand-delivered. I'm sorry I didn't ring and advise you.' She pulled a face. 'We had a sudden influx of guests who all wanted to know different things and book morning calls.'

'It's fine,' Sarah reassured her. She peered at the woman's name badge. 'Thanks, Kirsty. I'm going out for dinner but I doubt it'll be a late night.'

No way did she intend broadcasting her date with the manager.

'If the doors are locked, just press the bell. There's always someone on duty, Miss Barnes. Have a great evening.'

Sarah glanced at her watch. It was exactly seven-thirty. Before she left, she had to find out what her message was. It could only be from Morag, but she couldn't think what might be so urgent that it wouldn't keep until the next day. Unless something had happened . . .

She tore open the envelope, her heartbeat upping its rhythm as she read Rory's note. Briefly she closed her eyes. Given her plans for the evening, and what she'd heard about the young doctor, this was potentially embarrassing, never mind totally audacious!

Sarah had no illusions about people's interest in other people's doings in smaller communities. Only Morag knew why she was in Kirlaig, but even those unaware of that long-ago situation might well wonder what was going on if they heard the girl from London had dated the manager of the Burns Lodge then gone out with the doctor who was their new GP and who'd had a steady girlfriend for several years.

Sarah realised she was jumping ahead of herself, but wondered why life sometimes became so complicated. Rory McLean deserved a scolding for trying to make a date with her when he was spoken for.

She stuffed the note in her handbag and let herself out of the foyer. Alistair stood near the exit gate and he raised a hand in greeting and walked towards her.

He was wearing dark jeans and a blue and white checked shirt. His hair had that straight-from-the-shower look, making him appear younger than he did when wearing his dark suit and with his hair tamed by gel.

'Hi. You look very nice.' He waved at

a sleek black saloon. 'Shall we get going?'

Sarah got the feeling he might not want to be seen taking one of the guests for a drive, but told herself she mustn't be paranoid.

'Of course.' She followed him and got into the passenger seat. 'You look very different when you're wearing casual clothes.'

'In a good way, I hope.' He got behind the wheel. 'Wearing a suit for work's fine, but it's great to relax when I can.'

They were pulling out of the car park and driving along the road she knew led to Fort Robert. Fortunately Alistair was talking about the village they were heading for, giving her time to adjust her thoughts because the place name he mentioned meant nothing to her, so probably wasn't the one where Rory left the train the night before. So much seemed to have happened since then.

'You've enjoyed your day, I hope?'

Alistair kept his eyes on the twisting road.

'Very much, thanks. I managed to track down an old friend of my grandma. It was good to find her still living in Kirlaig.'

'Wow, well done. That didn't take you long.'

'It was pure luck that I found her so easily.'

Alistair was slowing down behind a truck.

'So now you've found this person, do you think your grandmother will take a holiday in Kirlaig to see her old acquaintance?'

Sarah chuckled.

'Are you after more business, Alistair?'

'Well, it can never hurt to drop a hint! It would be great to see you come back again, Sarah, with or without your grandmother.'

'Well, thank you, but you hardly know me.'

'That's why I invited you out for the

evening. I'm hoping to get to know you better. I took the liberty of checking your room reservation earlier and I'm sad you're only booked for three more nights. Would you consider extending your stay? I'm due a full day and a half off later in the week.'

She wondered how desperate this man was for female company.

'It's possible. I . . . I might know more tomorrow, after I visit Morag again.'

'You don't mean Morag Lennox by any chance? The lady who runs the café?'

Sarah glanced sideways.

'How did you know that? Surely there must be several women around here with the name of Morag?'

'If there are, I don't know them. But Morag Lennox's date loaf is a legend in these parts, and if ever guests ask which the best tearoom is down town, I always recommend hers.'

'I love the way you say 'down town'.'

'Don't mock! You should see this

place once the tourists start pouring in.'

'I love what I've seen, but I'm not sure I'll be doing too much more sightseeing.'

'How come?'

She craned her neck to watch a gull wheeling and swooping towards the sea.

'Did you know Morag has injured her foot and she's having to wear one of those boot things?'

He whistled.

'That must slow her down, poor lady.'

'It certainly makes life difficult. That's why I'm wondering whether I should offer to help her out — just for a short while, of course.'

'That sounds very generous to me, but don't you have a job to go back to?'

'I'm between contracts at the moment. You'll probably think me very boring, but I work in IT.'

'Rather you than me,' Alistair replied. 'But you're not at all boring, Sarah.'

She decided not to respond.

'Another couple of miles and we'll be

there,' he said. 'Maybe you could tell me how your grandmother met Morag Lennox and what made you decide to come all the way up here to try to locate her. I'd be interested to know.'

★   ★   ★

Seated at a table with a view of the small islands off the coastline and sipping sparkling water, Sarah decided to see how Alistair reacted if she mentioned Cathy and Dr McLean.

After they gave their food orders, she sat back and told him how she'd spent a few days staying in Glasgow.

'But you asked what made me travel to Kirlaig,' she said. 'To be honest, it's a delicate subject, but I'm hoping to make sense of certain things and reassure my grandma her name isn't as black as she fears it might be.'

'This sounds like the start of a mystery novel,' Alistair said. 'Tell me more. I can assure you I'm used to discretion, being in the hotel trade.'

Sarah waited while the waiter served the glass of wine which Alistair had insisted would go beautifully with her choice of baked sea trout, potato wedges and salad.

'Many years ago, my grandmother took a job in your hotel, though I believe it was known by another name then?'

His eyes sparked with interest.

'Yes, they called it West Mount, but when it changed hands the new owners went for something they thought sent the right marketing message.'

She nodded and, choosing her words carefully, explained how her grandmother's stay had ended in tears.

Alistair listened without interrupting.

'As I said, it was a long time ago,' Sarah said. 'But I wondered whether you'd heard anything about a scandal involving one of the hotel employees. Probably not . . . '

'I haven't personally, but we do have a chambermaid whose mother and grandmother worked in the hotel before her. I could ask for you.'

Sarah shook her head.

'No, it's fine, thanks. I'm hoping to learn more from Gran's friend when I visit her tomorrow. I don't want to stir up old news and cause anyone heartache, so I'll be well pleased if any old gossip's long forgotten.'

Alistair sat up straight.

'I'm sure it must be, but am I right in thinking the GP in question belonged to the same family as Rory McLean?'

'You are.'

'I see. Which reminds me . . . Dr Rory left a note for you this afternoon, but I thought I'd better leave it to my staff to hand to you, rather than bring it personally.'

'Yes, I've received the letter, thanks.'

'And dare I ask whether the good doctor's helping with your inquiries?'

Sarah hoped Alistair didn't take her glare too much to heart.

'Sorry, that was out of order.'

'He probably won't want to know me once he discovers whose granddaughter

I am.' She watched Alistair's eyes narrow and wondered who he'd seen come through the door.

He leaned closer.

'Well, you may be about to find out.'

10

Out of Bounds

Rory had failed to interest his father in joining him and his sister Alex for a meal up the road in their favourite pub restaurant. Will McLean, while his wife was working away from home, was trying to catch up with a box set of a series whose name rang faint bells with Rory.

'What was that thing Pa's so keen on watching?' he asked his sister as she drove away from their house. 'Something political, did he say?'

'Probably. He's been watching it on and off for ages,' Alexandra replied.

'I feel a bit mean, leaving him on his own, but at least we had lunch together at Nana's.'

'He's happy. He's got you back, and you'll be staying with the folks for a while, I imagine?'

'If they'll have me. Nana reminded me I need to think about moving into the doctor's flat on her top floor.' He hesitated. 'Tradition — I know Pa lived there when he was a bachelor boy.'

They drove on in silence for a while before Rory decided to broach the subject of his failed romance.

'This is good. Just the two of us coming out gives us a chance for a proper talk.'

'You mean about you and Fiona?' Alex changed gear as the road flattened out. She drove on steadily.

Rory fixed his gaze on the sunset.

'Nothing beats this place. For the big skies — or for the gossip. I suppose she's already told you about Andy and her getting together?'

'She's my best friend, big bro. Of course Fi's told me everything.'

'She didn't actually tell me until I turned up to see her this morning.'

'From what I gather, you two were drifting and it was only a matter of time before one of you decided to tackle the subject.'

'You're right, Alex, and we all know it's for the best. When Fi came out to Boston we had lots of fun, but it was rather like a farewell, looking back at it now. I'm glad Andy turned up and the two of them sorted themselves out.'

'I'm hoping to wear the most beautiful maid of honour dress ever!'

'Let's hope they name a date soon. When did you say your boyfriend's due to arrive?'

'He flies into Inverness next Monday. I'm meeting him and we're taking a few days to tour round before I bring him home to meet the aged parents.'

'Don't let Ma hear you say that! She'll be back by then, won't she?'

'She will. And don't worry, Rory. I'll be the perfect daughter. I do so want everyone to like Jack.'

'He can't be too bad if he's in love with you.'

'You didn't say that when I was

fifteen and had that crush on the vicar's son.'

'Ah, yes. I remember him — the boy with the hair.'

'And what about you, Rory? Do you have your eye on a replacement for my best friend? Did you leave a trail of broken hearts in Boston?'

He pondered. Dare he mention the girl on the train? Probably not — but he couldn't resist taking his mobile phone from his pocket to check for messages.

'I booked a table for eight-fifteen,' Alex said. 'We're a little early.'

'As you so kindly offered to drive us, I can enjoy a wee dram.'

'Make the most of it,' she said. 'Once you start work officially . . . '

'I know, I know! No crafty wee tipple on school nights.'

Alex drove around the side of the Lobster Pot restaurant and into a parking space.

'Come on,' she said. 'I'm starving.'

The first person Rory noticed when he held the door open for his sister, was the hotel manager he'd met earlier. And from what he could see of the young woman sitting with her back to the door, Mr Murray's companion was Sarah Barnes.

Alexandra was heading for the bar to announce their arrival. Rory hesitated, stuck between being polite and greeting the other couple, or doing what he really wanted to do, which was slink away to join his sister and hope their table was nowhere near Murray and his guest.

Still, he knew where he stood now. Sarah had ignored his invitation to contact him, probably because the hotel manager had seized the moment, leaving Rory out in the cold.

Rory's sister was chatting to the proprietor while he prepared her lime and soda with crushed ice. Rory, left feeling as though someone or something was crushing his chest, decided this situation was ridiculous and he needed to face his demons.

At once he headed for the window

table where the hotel manager and Sarah were enjoying the evening sunshine.

'Good evening, Doctor McLean.' Alistair rose immediately. 'You know my guest, I think?'

'We've met, yes. Hello, Sarah. Good to see you both again.'

'Rory.'

She looked so beautiful. But what right did he have to think of her like that? Rory smiled through frozen lips.

'I won't disturb your evening any further. Enjoy your meal.' He turned away and strode towards the bar.

'Can you see who he's with?' Sarah whispered to Alistair. 'Is it his girlfriend or his sister?'

'Search me! I don't know any of the McLean women except for the present GP's wife who must be Rory's mother. But I bet you our waiter will know who's who. Why don't you ask him when he brings our meals?'

'No, no, it's all right. I was . . . I was just wondering, that's all.'

Sarah gazed out at the view. The restaurant overlooked a small cove and through the window she could see it was low tide and the silver sands were not only visible, but gleaming in that special evening light.

No wonder her grandma had fallen in love with this part of the world. But how could she stop herself from falling in love with someone so clearly out of bounds?

11

It Takes Two

Sarah hadn't slept well. She'd spent an enjoyable enough evening with Alistair, but couldn't help feeling he was a little too keen, considering she didn't plan on hanging around.

He'd gone a bit quiet after she tried to discover who was with Rory, probably sensing her interest, but luckily the arrival of delicious plates of food had soon changed the atmosphere back to a pleasant one.

She'd decided not to quiz the waiter about Rory's companion, but Alistair lost no time in checking so she knew the attractive girl whose hair was a shade darker than Rory's was his sister and that she taught in an Edinburgh school. But even though he hadn't been escorting his girlfriend to dinner, she definitely existed.

Sarah opted for a continental breakfast, thinking it might be good to support Morag's lunchtime trade later. She needed a chat and she was determined to offer her help, even if it was turned down.

She was crossing the foyer towards the staircase when the duty receptionist called her name.

'I was about to ring your room, Miss Barnes. I have a call for you. I'll put it through to the desk extension if you like.'

'That's fine, thanks.' Briefly Sarah wondered about Cathy, miles away in London, and sucked in her breath, hoping this wasn't some kind of emergency.

She picked up the phone.

'Sarah speaking.'

'Sarah. It's me, Rory.'

If only he didn't sound so gorgeous.

'Hi. I didn't expect to hear from you again.'

There was silence for a few seconds

before he spoke.

'Does that mean you'd prefer me not to contact you?'

She didn't stop to think.

'Rory, what's going on here? I wanted to get in touch, but under the circumstances, I decided I'd be making a huge mistake.'

'Why? What circumstances are these?'

Was this man totally lacking in common sense, not to mention commitment?

'The little matter of your girlfriend, Doctor McLean?'

His next silence was followed by a rich chuckle.

'Ach, how the gossip machine grinds on. I used to have a steady girlfriend, Sarah, but we are, as they say, no longer an item. When I gave you my card, I was on my way to talk to Fiona and tell her I thought we should go our separate ways. I was dreading it — arrogant enough to assume she'd be heartbroken. But as it happens, she felt the same, so the conversation was entirely amicable and I'm delighted to say she's found someone far more suitable.'

Sarah felt as though, having struggled to stay afloat, she was now swimming confidently across one of the glistening lochs she'd glimpsed through the train window. But the other problem still occupied her thoughts, and she had a feeling it wouldn't be solved quite so simply.

'Look,' he said, 'I know you're here on holiday, and this is going to sound ridiculous, but I'd really like to spend time with you. Get to know you a little better.'

She laughed.

'All right, but I have something to ask you. It's something to do with our families, so you've been warned.'

'Is this an ancestry thing? Please don't tell me we're related!'

'I'd prefer not to discuss it over the phone.'

'Then are you free tonight? Could I buy you dinner? Introduce you to another restaurant?'

'I'd like that very much,' she replied.

Once they'd made arrangements, Sarah hung up the phone and strolled down to the harbour before calling on Morag. She wondered if the café owner lived above the shop and, if so, how she managed the stairs.

After pausing to watch a bulging net of freshly caught fish being unloaded, and chatting to a couple she'd met at breakfast earlier, she made her way to the café.

The wee girl looked up as Sarah entered.

'Hi,' she said. 'I'm afraid Mrs Lennox is at the doctor's, having her foot examined. Would you like a coffee?'

'I'm good, thanks, Rhona. So, how's it going?'

The teenager screwed up her face.

'It's hard work. I like working for Mrs Lennox, but I don't know how we're going to cope now her sister's gone back south.'

'I've been wondering the same thing. What do you think your boss would say

109

if I offered my services?'

'Do you really mean that?'

It was Sarah's turn to screw up her face.

'I'm not the best when it comes to cake making. I always seem to forget to do something. Does it count that I love watching 'Great British Bake Off'?'

Rhona chuckled.

'Me, too. It's not my place to say, but I'd really like a chance at the baking — as long as Mrs Lennox is there to guide me.' She put her head to one side and looked Sarah up and down. 'But who would do the waiting?'

'I'll have you know I did plenty of waitressing jobs while I was away at uni. You'd need to teach me how to operate that scary coffee machine, though.'

'It's not as bad as it looks. And we make tea the old-fashioned way. Mrs Lennox won't have a teabag in the house.'

'Speaking of which, how on earth is she managing at home? Don't tell me she lives over the café?'

'Oh, no. She lives in a cottage along the bay. My mum drives us here in the mornings and collects us both at the end of the day. As soon as Mrs Lennox gets that boot off and the doctor says the word, she'll be driving again. Just now, she's using her front room as a bedroom. She's managing fine but fed up she can't do everything she wants.'

The doorbell pinged and a young family surged through.

'OK, Rhona, I'll hang on if that's all right. I must be able to help with something.'

The wee girl's mum delivered Morag back just as half the quayside seemed to have descended upon the café. By now, Sarah, hair tucked into a cap, was wearing one of the proprietor's overalls and, while Rhona dealt with the scary coffee machine and the tea making, was happily serving slices of cake, toasting and buttering teacakes and doling out scones with cream and jam.

The atmosphere was filled with a happy buzz, and though Sarah caught

Morag's look of astonishment when she first stomped through the door, it didn't take long before she was smiling with pleasure.

'You didn't have to do this, Sarah, but thank you very much. I can at least do the washing up, if you've time to stay a while. There's usually a lull before the regular lunch customers arrive, but with the tourists starting to show up, there's plenty to do.'

'I can stay. What did Doctor Mc . . . What did the doctor say about your foot?'

'Two more weeks then hopefully no more boot.'

'Well, let's have a chat later. And don't go overdoing it. I'd have thought you'd have a dishwasher.'

But Morag's response to that was a loud 'Huh' as she made her way to the kitchen.

As forecast, the busy period petered out almost as suddenly as it had begun and Morag had done a grand job in the back room.

'You really shouldn't be on your feet as much as you are,' Sarah scolded.

'That's what the doctor said, but this boot won't let me race around, and if I don't try to stand up and do a few jobs, what will happen to my business?' She called to Rhona. 'Make yourself a drink now — and one for Sarah, too. Help yourselves to a cake or something. We've not run out yet.'

She smiled ruefully at Sarah, but there was a suspicious moisture beading her eyelashes.

'Just coffee will be great for me, but I have a suggestion.' Swiftly Sarah outlined her plan, speaking firmly and ignoring the several occasions when she saw Morag open her mouth to try to speak.

'But have you no job to return to?' Morag asked at last.

'I'm exploring a few options but nothing's confirmed yet. What I could do with is somewhere inexpensive to stay for a week or two.'

'You could move in with me. If

you're really sure about this, that is? When my sister used my guest bedroom recently, she left it tidy and with clean bed linen.' Morag chuckled. 'She knew I'd be fretting if she didn't.'

'If you're sure, then that would be brilliant. I'm no good with baking, though.'

'Not a problem!' Morag smiled. 'If this wee girl's willing to give it a go, from what I've seen today, we have a team.'

'Great! I'll stay the remaining two nights I'm booked into Burns Lodge and we can sort out the rest later. I won't say anything to Gran until after I've spoken to Rory.'

Sarah watched to see how Morag reacted to this bombshell.

'You're in touch with him, then?'

'We're having a meal together this evening.'

'No! What about his girlfriend?'

'I asked him that and they're no longer seeing each other, except as good friends. I want to know what, if anything, he knows about Cathy and his grandfather's relationship. If he's been told my gran wasn't a very nice person, I have to put that right, don't you think? Then I can put her mind at rest.'

Morag shifted uneasily in her seat.

'Perhaps I'd better tell you that a while after Cathy left Kirlaig and people were picking up on the whispers, Lizzie McLean wrote to me, asking if I'd take tea with her the next afternoon. She knew I'd been good friends with your grandma.'

'You went to her house, I imagine?'

'I did. I knew she must have got wind of things and I wasn't wrong. She asked me outright whether I'd been aware of something going on, so I decided to tell her what I knew, which wasn't much. Your gran had gone back to England and to my knowledge all contact between her and Lizzie's husband had ceased. I described the whole thing as a passing fancy and assured her Cathy was . . . was . . . '

'In bits?'

'Back then, I probably said she was devastated or very upset. But I do remember saying she hated the thought of anyone being hurt by her actions.'

'By the look on your face, Mrs McLean probably gave you a hard time?'

Morag sighed.

'By then the poor woman must have known, or at least suspected, she was in the family way. She needed reassurance, not hints that her marriage could be at risk.'

'I can't believe my grandma could have behaved so irresponsibly,' Sarah replied.

'Have a little compassion, my dear. Cathy was hundreds of miles from home and working long hours. He was a good-looking fellow, also working long hours. I'm not accusing my old friend of misbehaviour. It was more like thoughtlessness.'

'Even so, I'm surprised they found opportunities to meet.'

Morag shrugged.

'Where there's a will, there's a way. Most marriages go through bad patches at times. None of us are angels. Your grandma has suffered enough. When you go back, you need to reassure her that her name wasn't blackened.'

'You want me to lie to Grandma so she can put the whole thing from her mind?'

'After all those years, it would surely be kinder, don't you think?'

Sarah nodded thoughtfully.

'Young Rory's grandad was equally to blame, don't you forget,' Morag continued. 'And if Rory isn't prepared to acknowledge that, then you'd be wise not to have anything more to do with him.'

12

On the Brink of Heartbreak?

Rory collected Sarah from the hotel car park at seven that evening. The evening was cool and she chose to wear a little black wool dress with sparkly dangling earrings. She'd draped a cobwebby sea green cardigan round her shoulders but wriggled out of it once inside Rory's estate car.

'You might jump straight out of the car again, but I can't stop thinking how much I want to kiss you. You take my breath away, Sarah.' Rory leaned towards her.

What could she say? Within moments their lips met in a sweet kiss. He kept his hands on her shoulders briefly before moving away again.

'You're beautiful. But I know I daren't rush you.' He kissed her once more. 'I'm taking you to a place a few miles further on from the restaurant we were at last night. Hope that's all right?'

'I'm in your capable hands,' she said. 'But I feel a bit uneasy about you and me, Rory.'

'Why's that? I was never engaged to Fiona, you know. It's months since she stayed with me in Boston, and believe me, we really are just good friends in the true meaning of the expression.'

'It's nothing to do with Fiona. It's about the link I mentioned.' Sarah hesitated. 'Something that happened many years ago.'

'Why don't you wait until we reach the Piper and then we can relax and talk whatever it is through? Something that happened years ago can't be that urgent.'

He's right, Sarah thought. Whatever happened or didn't happen back then is no fault of his or mine.

Sarah glanced at Rory's profile. He was an attractive man, but she needed to remember he'd returned to his roots whereas she was only passing through, even if she might be around a while longer than anticipated.

'It's very intriguing to think the pair of us are connected in some way.' He sneaked a sideways glance. 'But I'm looking forward to a pleasant evening.'

'I have no doubts about your respectability, Doctor McLean.' Sarah achieved a fair impersonation of a West Highland accent.

Rory laughed.

'I'm impressed. And I'm pleased you could find time to spend the evening with me.'

'You're all so friendly. It's lovely.'

'Hmm . . . so am I treading on Mr Murray's toes, dare I ask?'

'No way! Alistair had an evening off and I think he took pity on me. I don't have a problem staying in a hotel on my own, but it was nice of him to invite me out.'

'Indeed it was, and in his place I'd have done the same.'

She laughed out loud.

'Well, you're not in his place, but you've asked me out anyway!'

'Haven't I just? And I wonder why that could be, Miss Sarah Barnes?'

Sarah concentrated on looking through her window.

'Great scenery,' she said.

'Indeed it is.'

She knew he'd glanced her way again.

'I imagine it's important always to keep your eyes on the road when you're driving in these parts, Doctor?'

Another of those chuckles and she was longing for him to stop the car and take her in his arms. Longing for another sweet, tender kiss.

Flirting was all very well, yet she was painfully aware it would be easier for both of them if they didn't acknowledge the attraction between them.

But when they got out of the car, although her wish for a hug wasn't granted as they walked towards the restaurant, Rory reached for her hand, making her feel as though this was the most natural thing in the world.

He squeezed her fingers before opening the door for her just as Alistair had done the night before. But she hadn't held hands with the hotel manager and nor did she want to.

Alistair was also a good-looking man, but the pull she felt towards Rory was different and unsettling. If only she came without baggage. If only she could stop wondering whether he might totally change his attitude towards her once he knew the full story behind her visit. Her thoughts were full of contradictions but she couldn't help herself.

'If it's all right with you, I'll ask if we may go straight to our table,' Rory said once inside. 'The bar's fine, but I've spotted one or two familiar faces so I'd prefer to dodge the line of fire.'

'The price of fame,' she whispered.

The waiter seated them in a small alcove beside a window.

'If I sit back with my head against the top of this wonderful chair, no-one can see me pulling faces at you,' Sarah teased once Rory had ordered drinks and they were on their own.

'What are you like?' Rory tutted. 'I knew as soon as I met you that you were different. Different and rather wonderful. If I reach for your hand, will anyone notice, do you think?'

'If I reach for your hand first, no-one can blame you, can they?' She moved her hand towards the centre of their table, wrapping her fingers around his.

'You're an enchantress, Sarah Barnes.'

Careful, Sarah, she thought. Wasn't that what she'd accused her grand-mother of being when Morag spoke of an irresistible attraction? Was she, too, poised on the brink of heartbreak? There was no doubting the feelings sparking between Rory and her, but should they trust this sudden attraction?

The waiter was making his way towards them, bringing their drinks. She wasn't sure who broke away first, but the moment passed, and after they gave their food order, Rory raised his glass towards her.

'Here's to the future, no matter what it brings.'

'I'll drink to that,' she said, painfully aware how shaky her voice sounded.

'Now, tell me all about this mystery connection between us. I can't wait to hear.'

Sarah nodded, took a deep breath and felt as though she was about to jump into a deep, dark pool of uncertainty. How much had he heard? And if he was aware of his grandfather's past misbehaviour, how much did it bother him? Whatever his reaction, she owed it to Cathy to present her side of the story.

'I'm taking you back, Rory, to a time when most folks were far more strait-laced than they are nowadays.'

'You speak for yourself.' He grinned at her.

'When my Grandma Cathy was a young woman, she made the journey to Kirlaig to work the summer season at the hotel where I'm staying. She was employed as a receptionist and she became friendly with your grandmother, Elizabeth.'

At once Sarah saw the change in Rory's body language. He sat up straighter and she saw him swallow hard.

She twisted her fingers together, determined to continue.

'It looks to me as if you're aware of what I'm about to say next.'

'I'd prefer to hear it from you.' He met her gaze.

'Cathy told me how much she liked your grandma. What she didn't expect was to fall in love with your grandfather.'

'He should have known better!' Rory's eyes sparkled with anger. 'He was a married man, for goodness' sake.'

'Cathy should have known better, too. Her old friend Morag has explained to me, much more clearly than my grandmother did, how devastated Cathy was, how much she feared hurting Elizabeth McLean, someone who'd been kind to her and helped her settle in.'

Rory leaned forward and placed his hands over Sarah's. His eyes were filled with tenderness and a quiet glimmer of hope flickered within her.

'She went away because of this, didn't she? I gather your grandmother returned to England.'

'She had no alternative. She did the right thing because she understood very clearly how dangerous a situation had been created. She wasn't a bad girl, she was far from home and enjoying her job and making a few friends, like Morag and your grandma. It wasn't as though she set her cap at your grandfather.'

Rory smiled.

'That's a nice old-fashioned expression.'

'Morag's words, not mine. But I'm here not just to admire the magnificent scenery and do some seal spotting. When I was planning my trip to Glasgow, I decided to travel on to

126

Kirlaig because I knew Gran fell in love with the place, but when I told her, she blurted out all this stuff about her past.'

'Snap! A similar thing happened to me when I was at my grandmother's house for lunch. While we were waiting for my father to join us, I began telling her about you.'

Sarah's throat dried.

'Me? But why?'

He pursed his lips.

'Why do you think?'

'I . . . I'm not sure what to think.' Gently she withdrew her hands from his and took a welcome sip of her drink.

'Then don't try.' He spoke gently. 'My grandmother — Nana is what my sister and I call her — is aware Fiona and I are officially just good friends and she sounded very positive about my meeting you. But I made some remark about being determined not to become the subject of gossip and Nana looked so shocked I was worried I'd upset her in some way. Then it all came out, but I don't think too many people know about the affair.'

'I truly don't think it was an affair in the shameful meaning of the word. There was too much at stake for them to risk causing a scandal.'

'If that's your feeling I'm happy to go along with it. My grandmother was unlikely to go into details, was she? She must have been devastated at the time.'

'This is what's haunting Cathy. She worries that Elizabeth McLean still views her as . . . as . . . '

'You don't need to spell it out, Sarah. I understand why your grandmother feels as she does, and I understand why mine has such a fear of gossip. It's probably because of the line of medics in our family. Nana's view is that doctors should be beyond reproach, pillars of the community. Here's me on the verge of joining the family GP practice . . . ' He paused. 'It looks like our food's arriving. Now, stop worrying and leave things to me. I'll have a chat with Nana and put Cathy's position to her. I'm sure she'll understand. Trust me. I won't let this affect our friendship.'

★ ★ ★

'You're a sight for sore eyes!'

'Good morning, Alistair,' Sarah said as she approached the reception desk. 'I thought I'd better confirm I won't need my room after tomorrow night.'

'That's a shame. Can we persuade you to stay a little longer? Special rate? I was hoping we could take a drive together tomorrow afternoon.'

'Oh, I'm not leaving Kirlaig. I'm going to stay with Morag Lennox while I lend a hand with her café, but I'm afraid I won't be free during the daytime.'

His face brightened.

'That's an exceptionally kind thing to do. Maybe you'd like to dine with me tonight in the hotel restaurant, as my guest, of course.'

'Thank you, but I have rather a lot of things on my mind just now. I'm sure our paths will cross while I'm still in Kirlaig.'

'Could I ask whether a certain Doctor McLean is one of the things on your mind?'

She felt a little irritated and knew the manager had read her feelings.

'I'm sorry,' he said. 'None of my business. It's just that I'd hoped to spend more time with you, but I bow to the inevitable.'

'I'm not going to be around long enough to spend much time with anyone except my grandma's old friend and Rhona, of course.'

'Then I shall make sure to call at the café if that's what it takes.'

'That'll be great. Now, I'd better get going.'

'Have a good day,' he called after her. She supposed she should be flattered. Alistair was pleasant enough, but her brain was still reeling after her evening with Rory McLean. He was so much more relaxed with her now and she could only think his terse manner when she'd first encountered him was due to his anxiety over breaking things off with Fiona.

He'd banished Sarah's fears over the possibility of him deciding not to see her again — far from it! Now he knew she was remaining in Kirlaig for another fortnight, he'd made it clear he wanted to see as much as possible of her.

She'd be friendly with Alistair when he called at the café, but no way did she want to jeopardise her friendship with Rory by accepting a second date with the hotel manager.

She couldn't resist smiling as she set off towards the town's centre. The goodnight kiss shared with Rory before he'd escorted her to the hotel's main entrance still gave her a lovely warm feeling.

She shared his wish to meet up again and Rory had promised to ask his grandmother if he might bring her to the house so Elizabeth McLean could meet her.

Sarah's admiration for Rory was growing, and as long as she could subdue that little voice warning her not to become too involved, she'd be fine. Wouldn't she?

13

Words of Love

The café was still closed. Sarah rang the doorbell and waited for Rhona to let her in.

'You're good and early,' Morag called from behind the counter.

'I thought I'd try to make a good impression on my first morning.' She smiled at Rhona. 'I'm relying on you to stop that coffee machine devouring me.'

'You'll be fine,' Rhona said.

'The wee girl will put you right,' Morag said. 'Rhona, would you mind popping along to the pharmacy and asking whether my prescription's ready? Then we can plan our day, the three of us.'

As soon as the girl left, Morag turned to Sarah.

'Did you have a pleasant evening?'

'I did, thank you. I tasted pan-fried venison for the first time.'

'Is that right? And what did you think?'

'I wouldn't say it's my new favourite food, but I think it's great for a special treat. They served parsnip chips and different vegetables with it. Rory had the same.'

'And what about the most important item on the menu?'

'Well, much to my relief, Rory already knew. Mrs McLean told him only recently, but I think he feels, as I do, that it all happened a long time ago, so why not leave it at that?'

'Huh! It's all right for you young folk to say such a thing. Those of us around at the time can't dismiss it quite so easily.'

Sarah bit her lip.

'I know. It's for that reason Rory's going to ask his grandmother if I might visit her. He'll take me to the house so I don't have to face her alone.'

Morag looked stricken.

'Look, she can't eat me alive, can she?' Sarah felt anxious as she remembered how Rory described his grandmother's reaction after he mentioned the power of gossip.

'It's just that . . . in some ways I wish Cathy had let things rest and not confided any of this in you, Sarah — especially now you've begun a friendship with young Rory.'

'That's all it can be, though. Hopefully we can enjoy each other's company now and then while I'm still helping you out. After that, I'll be off home, never to darken your doorstep again.' She ignored the sudden sharp feeling of regret.

'Please don't say that. Just so long as you don't mind my West Highland terrier, you're welcome to stay with me as long as I've a puff of breath left in my body!'

On an impulse, Sarah got up and gave Morag a hug.

'I love Westies, and I'm sure there's plenty of puff left in you yet.'

'Well, one can but hope, my dear. Now, as soon as Rhona comes back, I'd like to do a stock check, then while I'm ringing my suppliers, you can have your first lesson on coffee making. And I was thinking, if you have a driving licence, what if I ring and ask my insurance company to add you as a named driver so you'll have transport? I'm being crafty, because it would save me asking Rhona's mum to chauffeur me around.'

'Go for it. I may as well earn my keep,' Sarah smiled.

*   *   *

The hours flew by. Sarah left the café at around six o'clock, able to operate the coffee machine — if not with full confidence, with sufficient expertise to get by. She'd coped while Rhona, under instruction from her boss, made trays of sultana and cinnamon scones. They'd come out of the range cooker looking golden and tempting.

Now, as she walked up the hill

towards the Burns Lodge, wondering how to pass her evening, her phone beeped, startling her. Why was she so jumpy? She stood still and checked her messages, oblivious to her surroundings.

'How did you get on?' Rory's message read. 'Can I see you later? My sister says she'll cook us supper.'

Sarah typed her response.

'How lovely! Should I get a taxi?'

Moments later, her phone rang and Rory was scolding her for assuming he wouldn't want to collect her.

'That's very kind, Rory, but if you'd waited until tomorrow night, I could drive myself over to yours. Morag's putting me on her car insurance.'

'I can't wait until tomorrow. How about I pick you up at seven? Alex says supper at eight. My father's gone over to my grandmother's as she has some friends visiting.'

'That sounds great. Should I wear anything special?'

'No, just something you'd wear for

an appointment with your doctor.'

Sarah resumed walking back to the hotel. It would be good to meet Rory's sister — hopefully much less daunting than being introduced to his father.

He hadn't said how Dr McLean senior had reacted to his son's broken relationship, but by the sound of things, it didn't seem as though Rory was in a position to speak to his grandma yet. They had time to arrange this meeting, of course, but the sooner it happened, the better, in her opinion.

* * *

After freshening up and exchanging jeans and blouse for a little green top and green and blue swirly skirt, Sarah went down to the lobby to await Rory's arrival.

The manager was on his way to the restaurant but hurried back behind the desk when he saw her.

'Ah, Sarah. I thought I saw the doctor's car appear on the driveway.

He'll be waiting round at the back. Here's what you requested. I think you'll find this a very acceptable white wine.'

'Thank you, Alistair.' Sarah almost said she wished he could join them for the evening. It couldn't be easy for the manager to enjoy much of a social life.

He seemed to read her mind.

'I'll need to find myself a date on the internet.'

'I hear it works for some people.'

'Maybe I'll bide my time.' He smiled. 'Better not keep him waiting. Seriously, I'm pleased you're having fun, Sarah.'

She hurried outside, determined not to blush. Rory was on his way to meet her. As if in slow motion, she walked towards him as he did likewise, arms reaching out to enfold her. They stood motionless, hugging each other until she tilted her face towards his and their lips met in a loving kiss.

Rory buried his face in the side of her neck.

'You smell delicious — like roses in the sunshine.'

'A couple of hours back, I'd have smelled of coffee and hot buttered teacakes. Probably with a top note of washing-up liquid.'

'Equally scrumptious.' He released her. 'Whatever will become of me? You make me forget everything!'

Again a tinge of anxiety shivered through her.

'I don't believe that for one moment, Rory — or 'young Rory' as Morag calls you.'

He burst out laughing as he opened the passenger door.

'Now that does nothing at all for my confidence. She probably still thinks of me as a ten-year-old touting for chores.'

'I'm sure she has the utmost faith in you,' Sarah reassured him.

She waited for him to settle himself beside her and start the engine. He guided the car through the gateway, checking it was safe to join the road to Gairton.

They drove in comfortable silence for a while.

'This is really kind of your sister, offering to cook supper.' Sarah looked at Rory's profile. She knew she couldn't escape the fact that she'd fallen for him.

He glanced her way.

'Alex makes a mean fish pie.'

'Yum — except I'm eating much too well in Scotland.'

'Well, it doesn't show.'

'It's kind of you to say so, but I'll be afraid to step on my bathroom scales when I get home again.'

At once she realised her mistake. Weren't they trying to live in the moment and not worry about what might or might not happen once her stay ended? She searched for something to say, something more thoughtful, but the damage was done. She knew by his silence she'd hurt him.

'Rory, I'm sorry. That was a thoughtless thing to say.'

'No more thoughtless than my comment. I . . . oh, Sarah, I'm falling in love with you and I know it's ridiculously soon to tell you how I feel, but if you only knew how you've turned my life upside-down, you'd understand. We McLeans are not generally known for being impetuous. We mull over matters rather than make hasty decisions. I'm sorry.'

'I'm not,' she said.

'Not what?'

She sneaked a sideways glance but, give him his due, he was focusing on the road, now and then glancing at the rear view mirror, both hands perfectly positioned on the steering wheel. Hadn't Morag described him as a steady pair of hands when talking about him returning to Kirlaig to follow the family tradition?

'Sarah?'

He's not going to let me off the hook, she realised.

'All right then, Rory. I'm not sorry that you have feelings for me.'

'Why do I sense there's a big 'but' coming?'

'Because we both know there can be no future for us as a couple?'

'I don't see why.'

'Surely it's obvious?' She folded her arms across her chest and glared through the windscreen.

'Then I'm obviously lacking in intelligence.'

'That remark's unworthy of comment,' she said.

'So, is it the men are from Mars and women from Venus thing?'

'Maybe. Oh, for goodness' sake, Rory, you're not the only one falling in love, you know.'

She saw the sign for Gairton's station ahead. They couldn't be far from Rory's home. Sure enough, he slowed down, indicated right and waited for a car to pass before turning down a narrow track. He brought the car to a halt and turned to her.

'Please tell me it's not with Mr Murray!'

'You know very well it's not Alistair Murray, nice though he is. It's you I'm falling in love with.'

Rory sighed.

'How long will it take, I wonder, before the pair of us stop talking about falling and admit we've already fallen?'

Sarah leaned in.

'Until you stop talking and kiss me again.' She closed her eyes, knowing he wouldn't disappoint her.

★ ★ ★

Rory, his arm around Sarah, pushed open the sturdy front door.

'Anyone home?' he called.

'Don't you lock your doors in these parts?' Sarah asked.

He chuckled.

'Maybe at night, if we think of it.'

'It's certainly not London.' Sarah looked around her. 'What a beautiful hallway.'

'It's great, but I can't wait to move into a place of my own.'

'Ha ha! We've yet to see how well you cater for yourself, big brother!'

'How d'you think I managed in Boston?'

Sarah recognised the pretty young woman who'd been with Rory at the fish restaurant, but wasn't sure if this was a handshake moment or time for an air kiss.

Alexandra came forward and gave her a friendly hug.

'Hi, Sarah. It's lovely to meet you.'

'You, too, Alexandra. Or should I call you Alex?' Sarah held out the bottle of wine, its gold-foil top peeping over the edge of the elegant carrier bag bearing the Burns Lodge hotel logo.

'Whichever you prefer. Thank you; this looks lovely. I'll away and pop it in the freezer so we can enjoy a glass in a while.' She rushed off.

Rory rolled his eyes at Sarah.

'She's a wee whirlwind compared with me.' He took Sarah's hand in his. 'Come through to the garden room and enjoy the view.'

'Would you two like a tot of malt?' Alexandra was back, eyes twinkling as she looked at the happy couple. 'Rory McLean, what were you saying about whirlwinds? People in glass houses and all that!'

Sarah felt happiness surge as Rory hugged her to him.

'I can't help it, Alex. This girl has stolen my heart.'

'So it seems.' Alex gave them both an appraising look.

'Why don't I fetch the drinks while you look after Sarah?' he said.

'Good idea.'

But the sound of the phone ringing stopped him.

'I'll get that on the way,' he called.

Sarah followed Alex through a cosy dining room where the table was set for three, and into an elegant conservatory with wickerwork lounger chairs and settees arranged around the walls. She stood still, gazing out.

'What do you think?'

'I think it's the most beautiful view I've ever seen. You have the sea, the sky, those dreamy hills in the distance and that ruined castle. Could I take a photo?'

'Of course.' Alex opened the French doors. 'It cools off quickly this time of year, but there you go.'

Sarah stepped outside and took two photos with her phone.

'Have a seat, Sarah,' Alex said when she came back inside. 'With my dad at Nana's, I'm hoping this isn't a call out.'

'Thank you. So is this the house where you two were brought up?'

'It is. We were both sent off to different boarding schools, but during the holidays we were each allowed to bring a friend back if we wanted, probably because our parents thought it would be less trouble that way.'

'It must have been idyllic, compared to living in London.'

'You've always lived in the city?'

'Yes, and I lived at home while I studied at uni. Now I've had a couple of years working, I'm thinking maybe I should do a teacher training course. I'm not sure where yet.'

Alex nodded.

'Rory said you worked in IT,' she said.

'It's a bit of a geeky thing.'

'Not at all.' Alex looked up as Rory entered the room. 'No problems, I hope?'

'It was my soon-to-be partner, checking on a couple of things.' He smiled at Sarah. 'Soraiya McGregor's worked with my father for several years now. I'm pleased to say I don't appear to have frightened her away.'

'Give it time,' Alex said.

Sarah listened to brother and sister bantering and picked up the glass of whisky Rory had placed beside her, taking a bigger sip than intended.

Rory looked at her.

'Are you all right?'

She nodded, unable to speak. The spirit had taken her breath away.

'You're not used to strong drink,' he said. 'It's a powerful malt, that one.'

He moved over to the settee and sat beside her.

'You don't have to finish it if you don't want to.'

But Sarah took a deep breath and discovered she rather liked the whisky's mellow warmth.

'We'll make a Highlander of you yet,' Rory teased.

'I'll just go and see how the fish pie's doing. I'll take my drink with me.' Alex left Sarah and Rory alone.

'Your sister's lovely.' Sarah took a cautious sip from her glass. 'Fiona's her best friend, isn't she?'

He cleared his throat.

'They've been friends since primary school and they took the same training course. I can't recall telling you that.'

'It must have been Morag.'

He chuckled.

'Which means you know a lot more about me than I know about you.'

Feeling braver now, Sarah sipped a little more whisky.

'There's not a lot to know.'

'Only that you're an intelligent young woman. You're beautiful. Determined.

And you think the world of your grandmother.'

'Do you think yours will agree to see me?'

'I'll call in tomorrow and ask her. I didn't want to get my father involved in all this.'

'Does that mean some of your family know and others don't?'

'It would seem so. Personally I think that's how it should be left. Only those of us our grandmothers have confided in matter.'

'And Morag, of course. But otherwise, I agree.'

'We'll have this sorted very soon.' He placed his glass beside hers and took her in his arms. 'But meanwhile, let's enjoy being together, shall we?'

14

Bleak Future

After another busy day, Sarah drove Morag's sturdy car carefully from the cottage towards the town. This was her last night in the hotel and Morag had suggested she took a lift back to the cottage with Rhona's mum so she could start using the car.

Rory was spending time with his father and Soraiya, the remaining partner in the GP practice. Sarah knew this was necessary but, having not heard from him, couldn't help feeling anxious.

She parked behind the hotel and sat, trying to decide whether or not to send Rory a text message. It didn't take long before she decided against it. She wasn't hungry, as Morag had insisted she stayed for a bowl of leek and potato soup, and she was about to leave her car and go up to her room when her phone beeped.

'I need to talk to you, Sarah. Could we take a walk together, if you're free?'

Her tummy lurched as she read the message. She found it a little ominous for two reasons. A colleague or a friend might have written those words, though she was probably foolish to expect a row of kisses. But Rory made no mention of his grandmother and that bothered her.

She typed her response, screwing up her face as she wondered if he might think she'd been sitting, phone in hand, waiting for him to call. But this wasn't about playing games, this was serious business and she agreed to be ready half an hour later.

Dressed in jeans and light woollen sweater, Sarah left the hotel again and headed outside. Luckily, there was no sign of Alistair, as she was in no mood for socialising.

Rory arrived only moments later. He

was always punctual, though she doubted if this state of affairs could continue once he began his full-time GP role.

He leaned over to open the passenger door for her and she slipped inside. At once he gave her a swift kiss on the cheek. Surely everything must be all right? Surely her doubts were unnecessary?

'I thought I'd drive up the road and park at the observation spot,' he said. 'You know the lay-by?'

'I've taken a walk around there.' She glanced at his profile. He looked so serious.

'Is . . . is everything all right, Rory?'

'I'll explain the situation when we get there. Pa and Alex are both at home and I thought it best to go somewhere quiet, without waiters and inquisitive folk around.' He paused. 'Have you eaten?'

'Yes, thanks to Morag.'

'Good. And how are things at the café?'

'Busy as usual.' She struggled to keep her voice steady. 'Morag insisted I collected her car this evening so I drove it back to the hotel.'

'She'll find it useful, having you as her chauffeur. I hope it all works out for you.'

The tiny cold knot of doubt wouldn't disappear. Sarah sat in silence as Rory turned off the main road and brought his vehicle to a halt. No-one else was around. He turned to her and looked into her eyes, touching her cheek with one forefinger.

'Sarah, this isn't going to be easy for either of us. Believe me, I didn't expect the reception I had today. Let's go for that walk so I can explain.'

Sarah wished he would just say what he had to say, but he took her hand and led her along a winding footpath, taking them up and around the sweeping curve of the bay.

The evening was cool rather than chilly, but she still felt slightly shivery. Rory had grabbed a tartan rug from the back seat, and after a few minutes of walking he pointed to a rocky outcrop and headed for it, choosing a sheltered spot from where they could see the ocean. He spread the rug over the grass and smiled at her.

'I'm sorry I'm not wining and dining you, but I thought you'd appreciate not being kept waiting any longer than necessary.'

'Rory, please tell me what this is all about. I imagine it has something to do with your grandmother, considering you haven't mentioned my visiting her?'

He sighed.

'Let's sit down. I'm still wondering how to cope with the situation, but thanks for agreeing to see me, Sarah.'

'I'm unlikely to make arrangements and tie up the little spare time I have now that we've admitted our feelings.' She sat down and stared out to sea.

He sat down beside her.

'If I had my way I'd scoop you up and move you into the doctor's flat with me, but that's not about to happen.'

'I should think not! We hardly know one another.'

'We may not have known each other long, but I think we both understand what's happening to us isn't just a passing fancy.'

'Do we really? Rory, please tell me what your grandmother said before I explode!'

'All right, then.' He put his arm round her and she couldn't resist leaning against him. 'I called round this morning, knowing she'd be free. Nana made coffee and asked me when I intended moving in. I said I was trying to spend as much time as possible with you, because . . . well, because I didn't know how long I could keep you here.'

'What did she say to that?'

'She asked if I'd bring you to see her.'

'Well, that's good, isn't it?'

'Not really.' She felt his arm tighten around her waist. 'I said you were keen to meet her, and she asked why a lovely young girl would want to meet an old woman.'

Sarah closed her eyes.

'So you told her.'

'I did.'

She reopened her eyes.

'I wish you hadn't.'

'I thought it best to pave the way. I'm sorry. I never thought I'd see her so angry. She really does have a bee in her bonnet.'

'She's an old lady, several years older than Cathy. Remember how she reacted when you told her you didn't intend becoming the subject of gossip? We should have known how upset she might be. Do you think I should write her a letter?'

'In her current mood, she'd probably tear it up,' Rory said. 'How about we leave her to it for a few days?'

'What if I ask Morag to call? Except she can't drive at the moment so I'd need to drop her at the gate and lurk outside.'

'I could drive Mrs Lennox there one evening, but why do you think Nana would listen to Morag rather than me?'

'Morag's not family.' Sarah drew away from him. 'Even though it happened years ago, Mrs McLean must have been horrified at the thought of her husband being disloyal, and now, because I'm Cathy's granddaughter, she thinks of me in the same way. I'm a threat to her family.' She blinked away tears.

Rory kissed her cheek and hugged her to him again.

'That's rubbish. I'm single and free to make my own judgements. You can't be blamed for what happened back then. Nana's overreacting. I tried my best to make her listen but she refused.' He put both arms around Sarah. 'We can get through this. Neither of us is to blame and we shouldn't be made to suffer.'

She heaved a sigh.

'It's not an easy situation. I feel awful about it, knowing I'm not welcome here.'

'But you are! This will blow over, I'm sure. She'll see sense. I might ask Alex to talk to her.'

'But then Alex will have to know, and before you know it so will your parents, if they don't already. No, please leave things as they are.'

'If that's what you want, I won't argue. I'm going to be up to my eyes for the next few days, but somehow we must keep meeting.' He tipped her chin gently upwards and kissed her with such tenderness and longing, she knew she was on the verge of tears again.

'I didn't come to Kirlaig to cause trouble. You're about to move into a flat in your grandmother's house. You won't be able to invite me there. Besides, I can't stay with Morag indefinitely once she's properly back in action.'

He stroked a lock of hair back from her face.

'Don't take it to heart, Sarah. I'm not going to give you up, you know.'

But she couldn't help thinking their future now looked bleak.

15

No Going Back

Sarah checked out of the hotel next morning. Alistair Murray was at the desk and he had her account ready.

'I'm sorry you're leaving us, but I'd like to say I think you're doing a grand job helping out Mrs Lennox, and if there's ever anything I can help with, please get in touch, Sarah.'

'Thanks, Alistair. I've enjoyed my stay. I must remember to give the hotel a good review.'

'That would be great. I'll drop by for tea one afternoon soon.' He looked round to make sure no-one was close by. 'I don't suppose you'd consider coming out for a bite to eat one of these evenings?'

She was about to turn him down but something stopped her. He'd been kind to her and it was highly likely she'd need a shoulder to cry on.

'Could I get back to you on that? It's very kind of you.'

'Of course. Now, how about we keep your case at reception and you leave Mrs Lennox's car in our car park until you finish later?'

Sarah set off for the café, touched by the manager's consideration. She knew he had a soft spot for her, although he must realise the feeling wasn't reciprocated. Maybe it would be unkind to go out with him, even though she'd no idea how her relationship with Rory would progress. But the one certain factor in her life at the moment was her commitment to Morag. She was almost at her destination when her phone rang.

He'd kept his word.

'Good morning,' Rory said, too cheerfully. 'I can hear seagulls in the background.'

'I'm hanging around at the harbour. It looks like Rhona's mum hasn't arrived yet.'

'You don't have a key?'

Sarah chuckled.

'I'd have to have known Morag at least two years before that happened. It's not a problem. They'll turn up soon.'

'This is just a quick call to say I love you.'

'Well, me, too, Rory, but I'm still wondering where you and I are going.'

'Nothing's changed as far as I'm concerned.' He sounded hurt. 'Regardless of anything else, I'm afraid you're the one who needs to decide how long to stay here. You know I don't want you to go.'

'But if I'm not welcome, doesn't that tell you something? Can you really expect me to tolerate that situation?'

'One tetchy old lady? Would you really let her come between us?'

'I don't know! I really don't know what to say. I don't have a proper job. I'm staying temporarily with Morag. All good things come to an end, don't they?'

'I have to go now. Sorry.'

She was left staring at her phone, but Rhona was getting out of her mum's car and waving at her. Another day at the café was beginning.

★ ★ ★

Morag looked sharply at Sarah once she'd got Rhona weighing ingredients for Victoria sponges.

'Are you sleeping these nights? You don't look right.'

'I'm always pale. That's how we Londoners are.'

'Stuff and nonsense! You look ill. Is himself giving you a hard time?'

'I don't want to talk about it.'

'The McLean men are never easy to handle. Trust me.'

'Now she tells me,' Sarah muttered. 'I need to get on.'

Morag's eyes narrowed.

'Or is it herself that's the real problem?'

'If you must know, yes! Mrs McLean

has made a pronouncement. She obviously can't bear the thought of setting eyes on me.'

Around four o'clock, the café door opened and a dark-haired attractive woman, probably in her early forties, came in and approached the counter. Sarah had been kept busy — almost enough to keep her mind off negative thoughts.

Rhona was tidying up the cakes display so Sarah greeted the newcomer.

'Hello, what can I get you?'

'A pot of tea for one and a toasted teacake, please, and don't hold back on the butter, but please don't tell anyone I said that!'

As Sarah had no idea who the attractive dark-haired customer might be, this meant nothing to her.

'I'll bring it over if you'd like to take a seat,' she said.

The woman headed for a corner table, but spotted Morag sitting on her stool, writing another of her lists.

'How are you getting on, Mrs Lennox?'

'Not so bad, Doctor McGregor. Thanks to my helpers and Doctor McLean's efforts, of course.'

'That's good to hear.' The doctor looked at Sarah. 'I hear your latest helper travelled a long way to see you.'

Morag chuckled.

'She did, but little did she know what she was letting herself in for.'

'I'm pleased to hear all's going well. Now, excuse me, but I must check my phone.'

Dr McGregor settled herself at her table and focused on her messages. She looked up as Sarah brought her order.

'Hi, again, Sarah. I'm Soraiya McGregor. I've heard what a great job you're doing.'

'Thanks, Doctor McGregor, but who told you about me?'

'Who do you think?' Soraiya's dark eyes twinkled. 'Rory tells me you two met on the train from Glasgow. I never could resist a romance.'

It was impossible not to react to her friendliness.

'And did he tell you he was sitting in my seat?'

'No! You wait till I see him next. I hope you kicked him out?' She began filling her teacup.

'He was very polite, Doctor McGregor.'

'Please call me Soraiya. I imagine we'll be seeing each other at Rowan House later this month for the welcome party. Rory's coming home celebration?'

Sarah gulped. What party? Somehow she kept calm.

'I'm not sure about that, um, Soraiya. The thing is, I'm not planning on remaining here much longer.'

The doctor looked puzzled.

'Well, I hope you enjoy your stay, however long it is.'

The bell pinged and a couple came in, giving Sarah an excuse to retreat. The cloud of sadness she'd been fighting off was settling upon her.

Why had she got involved with Rory? If only she hadn't arrived at the point

166

when he was finally ending a long relationship he'd decided was going nowhere. All he'd achieved was a new but brief association that was also doomed not to go anywhere.

And what exactly had he confided to his colleague? She was becoming more and more angry, especially since Soraiya, who quite rightly assumed Rory's new girlfriend would be invited, had given away a secret Sarah obviously wasn't meant to know.

★ ★ ★

After supper, too restless to sit still, Sarah decided to take a walk. One thing she loved about this part of the world was the long, summer evenings.

Morag settled herself on the bed settee, feet up, to watch yet another old film, while Drummond, Morag's Westie, who spent most of his day with Morag's neighbour, seemed happy to accompany his new friend.

They followed the gentle curve of the

bay, eventually reaching a bench at the end. Sarah sat down to gaze at the choppy water. The last ferry was heading for its mooring and she smiled ruefully, realising she'd memorised some of the timings just by hearing customers' conversations.

She still felt dispirited, and when her phone's ringtone broke the peace, she half hoped it wouldn't be Rory.

'It's me again, I'm afraid, Miss Barnes.'

'You sound cheerful, Doctor McLean.'

'And you sound quiet.'

'I'm sitting on a bench, watching the sea with Morag's Westie curled up at my feet.'

'I wish I could be there with you but I'm sorting out a load of junk from my teenage years and dumping the whole lot in black bags.'

'Is this in readiness for your move?'

'Perhaps. I'm not sure yet.' He sounded wary. 'I might remain at home until things settle down.'

'I'm not sure this is a good idea.'

'What, me throwing out my trash? I can assure you it is.'

'I meant continuing to talk.'

'Sarah, I meant it when I said I wished I could be with you. You know how much is happening in my career and my personal life just now, and if we can both stay patient, I'm sure everything will sort itself out.'

'Maybe, though it's probably best I go home as soon as Morag's able to cope.'

'Don't decide yet. Please trust me. If we can get through these next days, we can make some plans. Does that sound good to you?'

'Rory, I wish I could say it does.'

'Have you changed your mind about me — about us?'

He sounds exactly like I feel, Sarah thought. Worried.

'Of course I haven't, but I'm not prepared to hang around here, making life difficult for you and your family. Once Morag stops needing that surgical boot, I'll be leaving for good. Please don't try to persuade me otherwise.' She couldn't resist revealing how hurt she felt. 'How do you think I feel, knowing there's a party planned for the man I've fallen in love with and yet he's not allowed to invite me?'

She closed the call before he could respond.

That didn't stop him from ringing her again. This time, unable to bear hearing him apologise, knowing how helpless he must feel, she switched off her phone.

Somehow she found her way back to the cottage, probably because Drummond knew his way home. It wasn't a long and complicated walk, but she felt as if she was fighting her way through fog. She still couldn't believe she'd been so grumpy, when Rory was so obviously trying to remain positive.

Of course she didn't want to say goodbye for ever. But to go on seeing him, enjoying the warm shelter of his arms, sharing kisses and cuddles, joking with each other . . . it would be like having a black shadow hanging over them while the days ticked by and still Elizabeth McLean refused to change her attitude.

It was difficult beyond belief, distancing herself as she was doing. For days, Sarah got up and drove Morag and Rhona to the café, worked a full day and returned in the evening. After supper, she read paperback after paperback, often unable to recall the title of the novel or its author. She found it unbearable to watch the old films Morag favoured, as they were usually romantic comedies. And she couldn't find much to laugh about.

One evening, having walked the dog, Sarah let herself into the cottage and freed Drummond from his lead. He scampered off to the kitchen to lap at his water bowl while she peeped through the sitting room door. Morag was still watching her film but glanced up.

'How was your walk?'

'Good, thanks.' She forced a smile to

her lips. 'Fancy a cuppa?'

'That would be great. There's ginger-bread in the tin with the daisies on, if you're peckish. I think Jane Eyre's just about to surprise Mr Rochester, so I'll be switching off the TV unless you want the news.'

'I'm not bothered, thanks.'

Sarah headed for the kitchen. She had a feeling Morag suspected something was up, and in her current mood she wasn't sure she could resist pouring out her troubles.

★ ★ ★

'Thanks for listening.' Sarah dabbed her eyes with a tissue and sat back in the armchair. 'I've held it all in as long as I could, but I don't know that I can bear this situation much longer.'

'I wish I hadn't needed to hear it,' Morag said. 'I wish Lizzie McLean could let bygones be bygones, but there's no escaping the fact she finds it difficult, if not impossible. I wish you wouldn't dash back to London. I'm enjoying your company and Drummond's a big fan already.'

Sarah gave her a watery smile.

'You're very kind, but as I told Rory, it's not pleasant knowing his grandma wishes I'd never arrived on the scene. And one of these days I'm going to bump into him. It's inevitable.'

'Young Rory chose to sit in the seat you'd booked. He followed up that first encounter, so why not accept some things are meant to be?'

'I have to accept Mrs McLean won't tolerate me at Rowan House. Rory's preparing to take over the top floor accommodation, even if he says he's not sure yet. I can't imagine he'll want to continue living with his parents and sister when he can have his own self-contained apartment and entrance. Why wouldn't he want to move there?'

'It's a tradition with the McLean men, I agree. But if he's there and doesn't need to meet his grandmother except when he's asked to lunch or

173

calling in to say hello, if you visited him, you wouldn't need to see her, either.'

'That's not the point. It's still her home and I wouldn't feel right going there. I know you're trying to help, but I have to go back to London.'

'I feel dreadful now, having kept you here because of my stupid old foot!'

Sarah shook her head.

'Not at all. I offered to help and I don't regret it. By the way, I rang Gran last night and she sounded really pleased I was doing my bit. She said you sent her a lovely letter and I'm to tell you she's begun her reply.'

Morag put down her cup.

'I thought writing to her would make breaking the ice easier after all these years. I suggested I ring her after hearing back so we'll be speaking to one another before long. We always did get on well.' Her face became dreamy. 'We used to go to some of the dances after finishing work. The word would get round about a Saturday night ceilidh in one of the villages' halls and we'd beg a lift from anyone who'd take us there. My goodness, we were wee daredevils in those days!'

'Did you ever have the same day off?'

'Only occasionally, but when we did, we'd sometimes take the ferry across the water and stay on board, drinking tea in the cafeteria. The crew became used to us after the first couple of times.'

'Can you remember exactly how Gran met Doctor McLean? Not at a ceilidh, I imagine.'

'He never showed his face at any I went to. If my memory serves me correctly, Doctor McLean was summoned after a hotel guest fell and injured herself while out walking with her daughter. The daughter had to hurry to the roadside and flag down a car to get help.'

'No mobile phones in those days of course. So what happened?'

'The driver helped get the lady back to his car then drove the pair of them down to the hotel. Cathy was on duty and she rang Doctor James, which was the correct thing to do back then. He turned up at the hotel, saw your grandma for the first time and, according to Cathy later, nothing was ever the same for her.'

'Or him, from what I've heard,' Sarah said.

'Doctor James ordered an ambulance to take the patient to Fort Robert Hospital, then he asked Cathy if she'd mind going along, too, so she could keep the lady company. No paramedic teams then, you see.'

'How did she get back to Kirlaig?' Sarah thought she could guess.

'Doctor James followed behind the ambulance, and waited for the consult-ant on duty to agree with his verdict. The patient was kept in for the night and Doctor James drove Cathy back. Apparently they started chatting and, well, that's how they got to be friends.'

'Probably it was quite daunting for

Gran, setting off like that and being alone in the back of the ambulance with the patient. I can imagine her needing someone to talk to.'

'Motor cars are grand places to hold a conversation between two people because nobody can overhear. But at that point, I don't think either of them would have discussed anything other than the accident or how Cathy was enjoying working in Kirlaig.'

'I still don't get how they found time to see one another.' Sarah frowned.

'They didn't have much opportunity, that's for sure. It probably made the attraction, the crush, or whatever you want to call it, something very special. Of course they were being foolish, but it makes me angry how, because of something that fizzled out decades ago, you and Rory aren't allowed the opportunity to get to know one another.'

'Please don't upset yourself, Morag. I've made my decision and that's an end to it.' Sarah got to her feet. 'I'll take the tea things through and wash them up.'

'Thank you, my dear. But when I told you the McLean men weren't easy to handle, I forgot to add, they are nothing if not loyal. Even if there are problems along the way, they usually find a way to solve them. Back then Cathy made the decision to walk away. James McLean buckled down and became a fine practitioner and family man.'

'And his son?' Sarah asked.

'Will McLean has coped brilliantly with marriage to an independent woman who has a career of her own. I'm not saying there's anything wrong with Sheena's way of going on, but without a strong, sensible partner like Will, that family wouldn't be as they are today.'

'So it sounds like Rory's father didn't prove hard to handle?'

'Och, he was a bit wild as a young man, but Sheena didn't want to know him for years until he eventually saw sense and began to court her.'

Sarah smiled at the old-fashioned word.

'You could say Rory was courting me, but it looks as though our romance was destined to be short-lived.'

'Don't underestimate me, Sarah, please,' Morag muttered.

Sarah, collecting cups and plates, looked up.

'Sorry?'

'I said, could you let Drummond out the back door, please?'

16

Crazy Decision

Rory stared at the patients' database. For the first time ever since qualifying he wished he wasn't a doctor, or at least not a doctor newly returned to the small town where he was brought up.

Doubtless everybody from his former primary school teacher to the pharmacist working down at the harbour knew by now that young Dr Rory had his sights set on the attractive English girl. That didn't bother him, but his grandmother's attitude towards the girl he loved bothered him very much.

How was he supposed to convince her he'd fallen in love, totally and absolutely in love, and that she was being unbearably stubborn by refusing to have anything to do with Sarah, merely because she happened to have arrived in Kirlaig to trace an old friend of her grandmother's? Sarah was totally blameless.

Yet, in Lizzie McLean's eyes, Sarah was tarnished. That's what she'd told him. He'd laughed, an incredulous laugh, only serving to fuel the old lady's anger.

'So you think it's funny?' his grandma had snapped back. 'You think I can forget how close Cathy, someone I thought of as a friend, came to breaking up your grandad's and my marriage?'

Rory hadn't been able to hold his tongue, although he felt ashamed about that now.

'That's so unfair, Nana,' he'd said. 'It always takes two — surely you know that? And Grandad was the local GP, for goodness' sake. From what I hear, it was Sarah's grandma who made the decision to leave Kirlaig. She knew trouble lay ahead if she stayed and nor was she prepared to jeopardise her friendship with you any longer. She understood Grandad's position and how difficult it would be for everyone concerned if she didn't leave. I think she behaved better than he deserved at that point.'

His grandmother's face had crumpled. He went over and put his arms around her, but she stiffened, causing him to draw back.

'How dare you! I can't stop you seeing this girl, Rory, but I don't want to hear her name mentioned in this house ever again. In any case, this is a young woman you've only known five minutes. Compare that with the years you and Fiona have known one another!'

At that moment, Rory understood exactly how much Sarah meant to him. She had arrived in his life at a time of change and somehow he must convince her he cared about her enough to want to marry her. No warning bells about hasty decisions rang in his head, despite Lizzie McLean's taunt.

He'd turned on his heel and left the room. If his grandmother wouldn't allow Sarah to cross her threshold, then he was forced to seek alternative accommodation. But first, he must break this silence Sarah had decided was necessary.

★ ★ ★

Sarah eyed her phone but didn't move.

'Those contraptions don't answer themselves, you know.'

She frowned at Morag.

'You don't pay me to take personal calls while I'm working.'

'It's almost closing time. For goodness' sake, take that call which I presume is from himself?'

Sarah pursed her lips, but plucked her phone from beside the till and pressed the answer button while retreating to the kitchen doorway.

'Thank goodness,' Rory said. 'I was on the point of visiting the café, but . . . '

'You have your position to think of.' Sarah walked down the corridor leading to the storeroom. 'I feel the same about taking personal calls at work. What can I do for you?' She hated herself for using such a chill tone.

'I've made certain decisions today and I'd like to discuss them. Will you meet me this evening?'

Sarah closed her eyes, her throat constricting.

'Are you still there?'

'I can't come out with you, Rory. When I said we shouldn't keep meeting, what part of that did you not understand?'

'I understand I have two extremely obstinate women in my life. One of them I've dealt with, though I prefer not to talk about it over the phone. The other one . . . well, I'm so in love with her that if she won't stay in Kirlaig and marry me, I'll have to find myself a job in London, won't I?'

* * *

'So, you can see why I agreed to meet him later. It's vital I talk him out of this

184

crazy decision, isn't it?' Sarah turned to Morag, who was sitting in the passenger seat.

'I have to hand it to young Rory,' Morag replied. 'He's not prepared to dance to Lizzie's tune and that must tell you something about his character, surely?'

Sarah drove away from the café.

'It tells me he's not thinking straight. Oh, what a muddle all this is. Surely he doesn't think I'll allow him to throw away everything he's worked towards? What he's proposing to do would probably break his parents' hearts, not to mention his grandma's. She must be devastated, poor lady.'

'Has he given her a piece of his mind, then? I'd love to have been a fly on the sitting room wall.'

'Well, I wouldn't, thank you very much. As for your question, I don't know exactly what he said, but he told me he'd dealt with her, whatever that means. It doesn't sound good.'

'I need to have a think. There must

be some way to stop those two locking horns. And when you meet Rory, you might remind him what he told me when I saw him at the surgery last,' Morag said.

'And what was that?' Sarah kept her eyes focused on the bus they were following.

'I asked him how he'd liked America. He said it was a fantastic experience and he'd learned a lot, but he could never see himself settling down anywhere but Kirlaig.'

Sarah swallowed hard.

'I'm not at all surprised to hear it, but thanks for telling me. If he left, all the plans for his return would come to nothing. He'd be letting down not only his father, who's wanting to cut down his hours, but also Soraiya, who's looking forward to working with him and to introducing some innovations.'

'Never mind all that. What about himself? Could you see him working in London?'

'He could work anywhere, surely? He

told me he did a stint in Africa a while back. But that, like his time in America, lasted for a year. He must have wanted to return to Kirlaig, or else surely he wouldn't have agreed to it?'

'Precisely.' Morag shot her a quick glance. 'He's following a family tradition and, as much as I hate saying this, it's down to you to persuade him not to burn his boats.'

'Just like that?'

'I never said it was going to be easy.'

★   ★   ★

Rory looked around the bedroom he'd slept in for as long as he could remember. It looked a whole lot tidier now he'd disposed of so much rubbish — old magazines going back to his school and university days, an ancient tennis racquet with broken strings — so much junk that his mother, and he didn't blame her, had shut the door on it.

He checked his watch. He needed to

shower and change. His father would be back soon from surgery. How would he take the news that his son had changed his mind and would not now be following the medical tradition? He grimaced.

Whatever his father said, he couldn't let Sarah walk away from him, not when he felt sure she shared his feelings. He had to convince her he meant what he said. He wouldn't let his father down — he'd stay on and take his share of the workload while the practice advertised for a new partner. Then he'd be free to find a position wherever he and Sarah decided to live.

Rory was about to head out of the front door when the phone in the hall rang. His father still hadn't returned, so he waited for the answer phone to click in, heard his mother's voice, and picked up at once.

'It's me, Ma. Dad's still at the surgery.'

'You sound as though you're in a hurry.'

'I'm on my way to collect someone, but do you want Dad to call you back?'

Sheena hesitated.

'I'll ring again later. I imagine he'll be in?'

'As far as I know. Is it something I can help with?'

'No, darling, it's just that I need to stay where I am for a few more days and I want to explain why. It's a brilliant opportunity, but I do miss him, you know.'

'I should hope so, Ma. He certainly misses you.'

'Will Alex be around?'

'She's off somewhere with her boyfriend but we're managing fine. Don't worry.'

Time enough for that when you find out what your only son has been up to, he added silently.

'Enjoy your evening. Anyone I know?'

He grinned.

'No, but I'm working on keeping her in my life.'

'Really? So it's serious? Goodness,

Rory, I mean it's not been long since you and Fiona were close — '

'Not that close, Ma. But I'll explain all when I see you.'

He put down the phone, wondering why his grandmother appeared not to want Rory's parents to know about the grudge she still held, yet she'd confided in him about past events.

He couldn't help thinking his parents would need to understand the reason behind his decision. But first things first, because he needed to collect Sarah and convince her that while he loved and respected his grandmother, no way would he allow her to determine his future.

17

So Much at Stake

Morag received a warm, friendly letter in response to the one she'd written to Cathy. She held the letter in her hand now, having pulled it from her handbag after the young couple set off for their dinner date.

There had been no mistaking the happiness on Sarah's face when Rory arrived to collect her. Morag's supper of fresh salmon salad awaited her attention, but first she needed to make a phone call.

Cathy answered on the third ring.

'Cathy, it's me, Morag. I got your letter.'

'How lovely! I can't tell you how pleased I am we're in touch again. I'm so pleased Sarah's been able to help you run the café.'

'It won't be long before I throw away that boot, thank you. As for Sarah, she's doing a grand job, but there's something happening that I think we should have a wee chat about.'

'Is this what I think it is?' Cathy asked.

'Yes. It's not life-threatening, but there's a lot at stake when it comes to a certain young couple's happiness.'

'I think I know who might be behind this. So, are you going to put me in the picture?'

'I'll do my best. When I'm done, you'll understand why I'm ringing. I think you're the only person able to stop a certain lady from making a disastrous mistake.' Morag launched into her story, speaking clearly, voicing her concerns, explaining the consequences of Lizzie's stance, but not putting the blame on anybody.

Cathy didn't interrupt, didn't even click her tongue or huff with irritation.

It was Morag who heaved a big sigh

when at last she finished her explanation.

'Thanks for not beating about the bush, Morag. But that's one of your greatest qualities and you're absolutely right. I know what I must do,' Cathy said.

'I didn't want to put pressure on you, but I can't think of any other way to deal with this.' Morag hesitated. 'Will we keep it secret from Sarah?'

'Is that possible, do you think? But if I tell her I've decided to pay Lizzie McLean a visit, I have an awful feeling she'll forbid me to travel. If I book my train tickets and a hotel for two or three nights, Sarah needn't know about it until it's too late to stop me.'

'You're very welcome to stay here, Cathy. I'm still downstairs on the bed settee.'

'Goodness me, you're also still recovering from your accident. You're very kind but, in a way, I'm looking forward to staying at the hotel. I never thought I'd hear myself say that but it's true. I hardly ever go away on holiday so my piggy bank can stand it.'

'If you let me know your dates, I'll make sure Sarah's not likely to cross your path. Would you like me to put in a word with herself at Rowan House? Or will you do the necessary?'

'I'll have a good think about that, but I'm wondering about turning up and giving my married name to that housekeeper you mentioned. Nobody except you knows it and it might get me into the house.'

Morag thought it was good to hear her old friend laugh, despite what lay ahead of her. Confronting the woman whose husband she'd once fallen for took courage. Fortunately, Morag knew Cathy possessed that in spades.

'When will you hope to travel?'

'Hopefully before I lose my nerve! But I have a couple of appointments coming up and my neighbour's cats to think about until she returns from holiday, so I'll buy my ticket for the earliest day possible and make a hotel booking, too. I'll call and let you know once it's all sorted.'

Morag felt relieved as she put down the phone. Cathy had, without any prompting or bullying, decided to do what Morag considered to be the right thing. Surely Lizzie McLean didn't really want to become estranged from her beloved grandson?

★   ★   ★

No matter how determined she was not to let Rory back into her life, Sarah found it difficult. For a start, she was unable to resist thinking about him when she settled down in bed at night. Again, she knew he'd be smiling at her when she opened her eyes in the morning, his eyes sparkling and making her want to reach out to him.

She'd missed several of his calls to her mobile before she eventually spoke to him, and still didn't know why she'd agreed to go out with him again when, in the long run, it could only drag this miserable situation out longer . . .

Rory knocked on Morag's door and Sarah emerged without delay. They greeted one another and he drove away from the cottage in silence. Neither of them seemed inclined to open a conversation, but when Rory reached across and squeezed Sarah's hand, despite her best intentions, she clung on.

'I have missed you so much,' he said, raising her hand to his lips. 'Dare I hope you missed me, too?'

'Rory, you know I have, but what's the point in torturing ourselves?'

'I have a cunning plan.'

'What kind of plan?'

'Let's wait until I can park up and we can take a stroll while I explain.'

'All right, I'm sure you're an excellent doctor, but I don't understand how you can find a magic cure for this particular ailment.'

Sarah stared straight ahead, wishing she hadn't made that weak joke, though Rory had laughed at it. He seemed very sure of himself, but she wanted no part in his alienation from his grandmother, something that would surely cause his family to take sides, only causing further heartbreak.

A few miles along the road, Rory slowed and pulled into a lay-by. From the car they had a good view of the sound, the sea gently rippling as though giant invisible fingers trailed through it.

Cocooned inside the car, Sarah felt safe. It felt right, being beside Rory in a little world of their own making. After all, they were two adults, more than capable of making their own decisions. Each knew they wanted their relationship to deepen and last.

Yet, through no fault of her own, she was bound to hurt the man she loved. It didn't help her willpower when he turned to her and raised his hand to stroke her cheek.

She couldn't stop blinking as tears threatened to form, but Sarah knew what she must say to him. Somehow she struggled through.

'So, that's it, then? You're not even prepared to have a trial separation while we each stay at home and wait for the dust to settle? I can't bear the thought of losing you, Sarah, and I don't believe you when you say it's all over between us. Won't you let me come down to London for a weekend soon so we can talk again?'

Sarah was unable to face going anywhere to eat and they hadn't even got as far as taking a walk. She didn't trust herself to speak without letting down the barriers, and Rory, obviously recognising the futility of further protest, started up the car and drove her back to Kirlaig without saying a word.

He must be aware how distressed she was. They'd already said what they had to say. There was no way she'd allow him to change his career plan because of her. He'd failed to convince her he could live with himself if he chose her above his obligations, and she wasn't prepared to be the reason for Rory to disappoint his family.

She knew she'd be on her way home in a few days from now, and all she could think of as they neared their destination was getting away from Rory so she could no longer feel this anguish.

'I'd like to be dropped off at the hotel, if you don't mind.'

'Whatever you wish.'

Silence again. To give him his due, he made no snide comment about Alistair Murray and his interest in her. Rory was and would never be anything less than a gentleman. That's why she couldn't bear to allow him to cause pain to the grandmother who loved him so dearly.

'Nana will come round, Sarah,' he said, as if reading her thoughts. 'If I tell her I'm leaving Kirlaig because of her stubbornness, she'll see sense, I know she will, especially when I insist on my parents knowing what's behind all this.'

Sarah shook her head.

'Please don't use emotional blackmail on her, Rory. And her secret is not for you to disclose to anyone. To be honest, I think it could take for ever for her to change her mind. I need to find work. I can't expect Morag to keep me on, as well as Rhona, once she's fully fit. Either your father or Soraiya will be signing her off soon and, when that happens, I'll be returning to London as soon as possible.'

One swift glance showed the tension in his jaw, the grim expression on his face. He gave a curt nod and before long he was driving up the slope to the hotel's front door.

'Don't say goodbye, Sarah. Just please don't say goodbye.'

She understood. If she let him give her one farewell kiss, she'd be incapable of holding on to the stern resolve keeping her together.

She was out of the car and through the revolving doors to the hotel foyer before either of them could say another word.

18

Secret Plans

Sarah made for the bathroom, knowing her face was contorted. Tears were rolling down her cheeks, and she dreaded bumping into anyone.

As if on autopilot, she splashed her face with cold water, tidied her hair and made herself walk to the bar, planning to order a drink and try to pretend her world hadn't just ended.

'Hey! Good to see you.' Alistair Murray stood in the foyer, immaculate in his dark suit, arms folded across his chest. He hurried towards her. 'Are you meeting someone or can you spare a few minutes?'

'Good to see you, too.' Guiltily she remembered her promise to contact him. 'I'm sorry I haven't been in touch, but things have been hectic.'

'Life at the teashop must be full on.' His eyes sparkled with mirth. 'But I shouldn't tease you, should I?'

Suddenly his expression changed.

'Forgive me, but you look as if the end of the world's about to happen.'

'I feel it already has.'

He frowned.

'Could you give me a few minutes, then I can join you in the bar if that's all right?'

She was beginning to feel numb.

'Of course.'

'Order a drink on my account and tell the barman I'm on my way.'

True to his word, he arrived five minutes later as Sarah was taking a sip of malt whisky, holding the glass with both hands because her fingers trembled so. He headed to the bar and waited for a glass of sparkling mineral water to be served, carrying it over to her table.

'Now, what's this all about? Unless I'm butting my big nose in where I shouldn't?'

'No, it's good to have someone to talk to. I've . . . Oh, Alistair, I've just told Rory we mustn't ever see one another again. It's all over between us before it's hardly begun.' She sniffed and looked down at her hands.

Alistair reached into his jacket pocket and produced a snowy-white cotton handkerchief.

'Here you go. Ladies' handkerchiefs are only fit for dolls. And you don't need to return it. I must have at least four dozen of the blessed things.'

'In case any of your female guests dissolves in a fit of the vapours?' She blew her nose and gave him a watery smile.

'Christmas gifts from aunts can be rather unimaginative. I have every colour you can think of, but I stick to white with business suits. Now tell me all about it. Has Doctor McLean been a bad boy?'

'Not at all. The thing is, he's obstinate as his grandmother and he thinks I'm just as stubborn as she is, too, so it's a battle of wills, I'm afraid. As things stand, I'm out of here soon, probably on the Monday morning train.'

Alistair drank a mouthful of water and put down his glass.

'I could murder a beer,' he said. 'What if you had the chance of a job, Sarah? Would that influence your decision?'

She stared at him.

'I'm not sure I want to stay, knowing Rory is in and out of Kirlaig and risking seeing him when that's the last thing I want.'

'I don't believe that for one minute, and I know you already love the area,' Alistair said gently. 'It sounds to me as if you don't really want to leave but you feel you have no alternative. Am I right?'

Sarah nodded, too choked up to speak.

'Now, listen. One of my reception team has handed in her notice. She's on a short-term contract but she wants to be released as soon as possible so she can fly to Spain to join her boyfriend, so I need to get on the case. Would you like to be interviewed for the position? I don't have full say in the hiring and firing. My team leader would be present at your interview.'

'Alistair, it's kind of you to think of me, but I've never worked in a hotel.'

'You must have first-rate computer skills, which are interchangeable, so you'd soon get used to our systems. You have a pleasant manner — think how good you are at selling cakes! Speaking of which — what about that little café down by the quayside, with the prettiest waitresses in town? Could your boss cope without you or is she still walking wounded?'

'I think Morag's next and hopefully final appointment is tomorrow, though she'll still be having some outpatient treatment for a while. It'll make life easier for her when she can go back to her full role.'

'And she's not expecting you to stay

for the rest of the summer?'

'Definitely not. Morag would never dismiss the wee girl, as she calls Rhona, and she couldn't afford to pay both of us the going rate. They'll be fine.'

'We have separate accommodation for our live-in staff. If you were to get the job, you could work the summer season. That would give you time to address whatever's rocked the boat for you and Doctor Rory.' Alistair hesitated. 'I wouldn't dream of interfering, but if you want a shoulder to cry on, I'm your man.'

'I don't know what to say, Alistair. I thought I'd made the right decision, but having seen Rory's expression . . . ' She gulped. 'He looked as devastated as I feel.'

'In his place, so would I!'

Sarah gazed into the distance.

'Maybe you're right. Maybe I need to give him more time to explain to his grandmother how much we mean to one another, even if she's bound to tell him it must be love on the rebound.'

'With respect, that's not for her to say. He must stand up to her and defend you, though I can't for the life of me understand why she's dead set against meeting you.'

'She has her reasons.' Sarah bit her lip. 'Alistair, regarding your job vacancy, I really don't know how long I could commit myself to it — if I were successful, of course. Could I have a little more time to think, please?'

'I should publicise the vacancy online tomorrow. Procedures have to be followed, of course. You'll be used to that, I know.'

'Of course. Maybe I just need to sleep on it. I promise to get back to you in the morning, if that's all right?'

'It's fine. I hope you'll decide to be interviewed, but it's up to you. Thanks for being honest. You can be sure I'll not mention your link with the McLean clan to anyone. As you say, it's a secret from the past and hopefully things can be resolved with a happy ending in view. I do hope so.'

She smiled at him.

'Thank you. I'll drink to that.'

★　★　★

Next day, Sarah felt much more in command of her life. Despite what she'd said about not wanting to see Rory, she longed to tell him she'd changed her mind about travelling back home, at least in the short term.

If Alistair Murray was prepared to give her an interview, and if his team leader also approved, she might soon have somewhere to live and money arriving in her bank account.

What was the alternative? A miserable train journey back to London, every turn of the train's wheels taking her further away from the man she loved. And then having to put a smile on when she met Cathy again, having to watch her grandma's expression when she couldn't find the words to reassure her she'd made contact with Lizzie McLean and all was well.

Sarah used her mobile to ring the hotel after Morag asked if she'd mind going to the bank to fetch change for the till.

She stood in a corner of the bank's foyer, staring up at a portrait of some unknown person who looked as though he'd escaped from a Charles Dickens novel, while she waited to be put through to the manager.

'You're an early bird,' Alistair said at last.

'Well, I wanted to tell you I'd like to be considered for the job.'

'Excellent news. Right, Sarah, I'll need your CV to show my colleague, so the sooner you drop it in or e-mail it the better. You'll find a staff section on our website.'

'Thank you. I'll see to that today.'

Sarah walked towards one of the counter clerks. As she placed the bags of coins inside the satchel, she resolved to drive back to Morag's cottage on her break, where she could look up her CV on her laptop and send it to Alistair.

She turned around to leave the bank and walked straight into the arms of Rory.

They stared at one another, neither speaking, until Sarah broke the silence.

'Can you forgive me?'

'Forgive you for what? You're entitled to be upset.'

'I didn't mean to hurt you, but I know I did.'

'Look, we need to get out of here. I can come back later.' He took her free hand and guided her out, much to the amusement of the nearest counter clerk.

'Now,' he said, once they stood on the pavement. 'I thought we'd said all we had to say. Can you still look me in the eye and tell me we're finished.'

She shook her head.

'I can't. I was stupid, thoughtless and far too hasty and I'm sorry. That's why I asked whether you could forgive me.'

He took a step closer.

'I forgive you, if it makes you feel better. But it doesn't make the situation any easier, does it? I'm lunching with my grandmother today. I rang to say I needed to talk to her again.'

'But if she still won't listen, what will you do then?'

'I won't trot meekly away and pretend nothing's happened. I'll stick to what I decided to do, which is find a position that will enable us to see one another.'

'Listen, Rory. I've been offered an interview for a job at the hotel and I've decided to go for it. If I'm successful, I'll have accommodation and a wage for the next few months. It . . . it would give us time. If you think that's a good idea, of course.'

'Do I? Sarah, if you told me you'd be driving an ice-cream van around all summer, I'll be thrilled. It's a wonderful idea, but I won't take you in my arms and kiss you until we're on our own. Can we meet this evening?'

'Yes, please. You can text me later but I must get back now. And maybe it's best if you don't tell your grandma I'm not about to leave Kirlaig. I haven't got that job yet. Now, I must get back. We can talk later.'

★ ★ ★

Sarah was coming downstairs, ready for Rory to collect her, when she heard Morag chuckling.

Did she have company? No, it sounded as if she was speaking on the phone.

Sarah wandered out to the kitchen so she couldn't eavesdrop, then waited until she heard the sound of the receiver being replaced.

Morag stood in front of the fireplace, still in her work clothes and wearing a pair of fluffy slippers. She looked a little pink in the face.

'I didn't want to disturb you,' Sarah said. 'It's so good to see you with matching feet. Do you miss your moon boot?'

'I'm not denying I'm pleased to see the back of it, although it served a purpose. But look at you, all dolled up! You told me you were seeing young Rory again this evening so I imagine you've decided to make the best of things? I hated to see you so upset yesterday.'

'I must have been such a pain. I didn't want to say anything before, but I'm hoping to remain in Kirlaig for at least a few months.'

'Now that is good news. You know you're welcome to stay here.'

'I know. But if I get the job I've applied for, I'll be living in.'

Morag stiffened.

'I don't understand.'

'Alistair Murray needs a receptionist and he's offered me an interview.'

'Mr Murray at the Burns Lodge?'

'That's the one. If I get it, do you think my grandma will come up and visit me?'

But Sarah dashed back to the kitchen to fetch a glass of water. Her hostess appeared to be suffering from a sudden coughing fit.

19

Challenges Ahead

'Ask himself to step inside,' Morag called as the doorbell rang.

'Is he in trouble?' Sarah called over her shoulder.

'Never you mind!'

Sarah opened the front door and beckoned to Rory.

'Morag wants a word.'

He gave her a swift kiss on the cheek. 'You look gorgeous.'

'Thank you. I'm a lot happier than I was twenty-four hours ago,' she said, leading the way.

'Mrs Lennox.' Rory beamed as he entered the sitting room. 'Got your feet up, I'm pleased to see.'

'Your father pronounced me fit for purpose. Is that the right expression?'

'It'll do well.'

'How is Elizabeth?' Morag asked. He hesitated.

'I realise you two go back a long way. You'll understand Nana hasn't made life too easy for Sarah and me, but I still can't make her understand that she's held a grudge for long enough. I wish I could make her see sense.'

Morag gave him what Sarah privately called one of her hard stares.

'Sometimes things need a while to fall into place, so don't be too downhearted. Sarah tells me she hopes to stay on over the summer and that means you two can get to know each other better.'

Rory grinned.

'Aye, if our shifts will allow it, we should get the odd hour or two here and there!'

'It'll be a lot easier than it would if this lassie was hundreds of miles away,' Morag reminded him. 'By the way, I might be asking your grandmother if I may call on her one of these days. Do you think she'll allow that?'

He raised his eyebrows.

'Of course she will. Dare I ask if you intend saying anything about Sarah and me?'

Morag tapped her nose.

'That, young Rory, is for me to know. Now, away with the pair of you and enjoy your evening. I'm going to watch a Cary Grant film.'

'She still treats me as though I was ten years of age,' Rory muttered as he and Sarah let themselves out.

'I'd no idea she was contemplating visiting Rowan House. I wonder if she really is going to try to talk your grandma round. I assume it didn't go too well for you today?'

He hugged her to him before she got into his car.

'She was flummoxed, I think, when I said things between her and me couldn't ever be the same again.'

'I hope you didn't frighten her.' Sarah said anxiously.

'You, Sarah Barnes, are an angel. No, I didn't frighten her, but I think she got the message when I told her I wasn't planning to move into the apartment yet.'

'I expect she blames me for that.'

Rory lifted her hand and kissed it before starting the engine.

'My guess is she has plenty to think about. She must be curious about you. If only I could get you two together, I know she'd love you.'

'It doesn't seem likely that'll happen, but I feel much calmer about it now, Rory. I know I want to be with you.'

'That's such a relief. Now it's up to Morag to see if she can work a miracle.'

* * *

Sarah insisted on driving Morag into town next morning.

'You mustn't expect to rush back to normal life just yet,' Sarah said, 'especially while I'm happy to drive you.'

'I'll make the most of having you around. When's your interview?'

'This evening, and that was Alistair's idea. He said you'd only start rushing around without me to keep my beady eye on you at the café for the next day or so.'

'Huh! It's a long time since I let a man boss me around. But while I think of it, I meant it when I said I'd like to call on Lizzie McLean when I've given it more thought. I can drive myself, but I wonder, would you be happy to keep the wee girl company?'

'Of course,' Sarah replied, 'and even if Alistair offers me this job, I'm sure he'll understand I can't drop everything. I'd prefer to hang around with you for another few days.'

'That's very nice of you, Sarah. It's much appreciated, though I'm not so good with flowery words.'

'I don't expect them.' Sarah decreased her speed, spotting cyclists ahead. 'What I don't expect is for you to upset yourself, visiting Mrs McLean. Rory says you'll give as good as you get, but I'm a bit worried.'

'Then you've no need to be. Herself and I haven't spoken much lately because she rarely comes into town, but I intend saying my piece, if she'll invite me over.'

'Do you think I should tell Gran the next time we speak? About you visiting Rowan House, I mean.'

Morag cleared her throat.

'I haven't got there yet. She gets plenty of visitors, so let's leave it for now, shall we?'

'It's going to be awful, telling Gran I'm not coming home like she expects. But if you can get through to Mrs McLean, it would make her so happy. I'm still wondering how to pluck up courage to tell her about me and Rory.'

'Dating the doctor?' Morag chuckled. 'It sounds like the title of one of those romantic novels the wee girl likes.'

'I'm glad you find it so funny,' Sarah said. 'Think what a double whammy it'll be, if I get that job. I'll be telling Cathy her only granddaughter's going to take over her old receptionist role, and guess what, Gran, I've fallen in love with Elizabeth McLean's grandson!'

She glanced at her passenger as she drove round the back of the café to park. At first she thought Morag was in tears, but clearly she was convulsed with mirth.

★   ★   ★

Sarah drove Morag back to the cottage after they closed the café for the day. She did a hasty freshen up before putting on a neat little green and blue shift dress, teamed with emerald green kitten-heeled shoes.

'You look very smart,' Morag told her. 'What are your plans after your interview? Another dinner date?'

Sarah thought Morag seemed a tad edgy.

'No, I'll come back here and fix something to eat. If you don't mind waiting, we can have supper together.'

'Oh, thank goodness,' Morag said.

'What I meant to say was I'm glad you don't expect to be out late. You've been working so hard lately.'

'I've enjoyed it. You know, maybe I'll give Gran a ring after we've eaten. It might be easier talking to her if I've got you here, too.'

'Oh, no, you mustn't do that!'

Sarah frowned.

'Why not? I haven't rung since last Sunday.'

'I, um, I forgot to tell you, Sarah. I spoke to Cathy last night after you'd gone out. Your gran said she was planning a week away, staying with an old school friend.'

'How weird she didn't mention it to me.'

'I think it's only just being arranged. She can't go until she finishes cat-minding for her neighbour.'

'Oh, I remember now. It's probably best I don't contact her at the moment, then, with all this business going on. I might upset her, don't you think?'

Morag nodded.

'It might be wise to wait a while, my dear.'

'OK. Is it Helen she's planning to visit? The friend she went to Paris with last autumn?'

'I don't think she mentioned a name. Sorry.'

Sarah glanced at the clock.

'Well, thanks for telling me. Now, I must go. See you later.'

★　★　★

'I think we've covered everything.' Alistair turned to his team leader. 'Unless you have anything more to add, Kirsty?'

The young woman eyed Sarah.

'Your qualifications are excellent. But I question whether Kirlaig's lively enough for you. I know you have use of a car, but after London, won't you find life here a little tame?'

Sarah coughed. Tame? She could sense Alistair's amusement as he gave his attention to the light fitting above his desk.

'If I'm fortunate enough to be appointed, I want to see as much of the area as I can, by boat and train. I also have lots of reading to catch up on. And I've made some friends who live locally.' She avoided looking at the manager.

'I know you've been a great help to Morag Lennox. Well done.' Kirsty smiled and turned to Alistair. 'No more questions. Now, if you'll excuse me, I must be on my way.'

He nodded.

'Thanks so much for staying on, Kirsty.'

'My pleasure.' She grabbed her handbag and left them alone.

'I'll be in touch after we've seen a couple of people tomorrow, Sarah,' Alistair said.

'Of course. I thought Kirsty asked some very direct questions.'

'She likes to play bad cop, good cop.' He rose. 'Now, I'll walk you to the door, if I may.'

'I'm parked round the back,' she replied.

'And I need to grab a bite to eat before I meet a guest off the Glasgow train. Donald's finished his shift so I thought I might as well collect this lady.'

'She'll be pleased, especially if she's come a long way.'

'Far enough. She lives in London. Told me she hadn't been in these parts for many years.'

'Then she's sure to notice lots of changes.' They were standing by the exit. 'Thank you very much for interviewing me. I'm off back to Morag's now.'

'No date with the doctor?' Alistair bit his lip. 'I apologise, Sarah. I didn't mean to pry.'

She shook her head.

'Rory has a duty dinner with his father and some friends. He told me it would probably be very boring, and his sister and I were better off not being invited, so I promised Morag I'd be back in time to eat with her.'

'It's good to see you looking so

happy. Speak soon.' He held the door open for her.

Sarah walked towards Morag's car. All of a sudden she remembered the party being planned for Rory. It was a while since Soraiya let slip what he chose not to mention.

Although Sarah now felt more secure regarding their relationship, it made her sad to think she'd be playing Cinderella while the family and their friends gathered at Rowan House to celebrate his return.

20

The Course of True Love

Sarah's grandma stepped down from the train and made her way along the platform. As she approached the exit, she noticed a tall, rather good-looking young man staring at her.

He lifted a hand.

'Would you be Mrs Catherine Carter?'

'That's me. Are you from the Burns Lodge?'

'I have the honour of being its manager, yes. Let me help you with your case.'

'Goodness!' She let him take over. 'It's me who's honoured, having the manager collect me.'

'Sometimes it's all hands on deck in the hotel industry.'

'You're so right. I worked in a hotel,

many years ago, so I know a bit about it.'

'I can imagine. The car's just round the side here so we'll be there in no time.'

'I used to take six minutes to walk back up the hill from the station.'

'Walk to the Burns Lodge, you mean?' Alistair looked curiously at her.

'That's right,' Cathy said. 'I worked a summer season as receptionist, back when the hotel was privately owned.'

'You'll be prepared for lots of change, then. I imagine you've seen our website?'

'I have indeed, and heard the bagpipes playing through my headset. How long have you worked for this group, Mr . . . it's Mr Murray, isn't it?'

He stopped and zapped his key to unlock the car.

'I'm Alistair Murray, and this is my second position as manager with the group. I've been here since last summer.' He hoisted her luggage into the boot. 'Now, let's see what you think of your former workplace.'

She chuckled.

'I doubt I could check myself in after all this time. We had no computer in my day — we just wrote everything down by hand and kept names pencilled in until the guests arrived.'

'I imagine you have plenty of memories.' He held open the passenger door.

'I have.' Suddenly it dawned on her. This was real and at last she was back in the place she'd left with such a heavy heart.

'Well, I hope you'll gather happy memories of Kirlaig on this trip. Don't hesitate to contact me, or any of my staff, if you need any assistance. You'll find we keep plenty of tourist leaflets and the like. How long is it you're booked in for?'

'I made the reservation for three nights, but it rather depends how things go.' She chose her words with care. 'I'm hoping to catch up with one or two people who still live locally and I have

228

some personal business to attend to.'

'We're not full this early in the season. I'll flag up your room so the team know not to book it out before checking with you first.'

'That's very kind.'

Alistair left his guest at the desk while he parked his car. Something was niggling at him but he surely must be mistaken.

Sarah had told him her grandmother used to work at the hotel, but this lady couldn't possibly be her, unless Mrs Carter was paying a surprise visit.

He shrugged as he headed back to the foyer. He wouldn't raise the subject with either of them. The ability to be discreet was a speciality of his.

★ ★ ★

Once in her room, Cathy hurried over to the window. There was that sea view with the little islands she remembered. If all went as she hoped, she could easily extend her stay, visit places she hadn't had time to see when working here, as well as spend time with her old friend.

Her tummy lurched as she thought of what lay ahead. She had made the decision to come because Morag had told her how fate had thrown the doctor and Sarah together, but she dreaded the thought of Lizzie McLean refusing to see her. She needed to ring Morag and hear her friendly voice.

'I'm so pleased you're here,' Morag said when she answered the phone. 'I can't talk because Sarah's due back. It seems so inhospitable not to invite you to supper, but — '

'We daren't give the game away! Don't worry about me, Morag. I'll order something to eat in my room. Am I safe to take a walk or is Sarah planning to come back into town?'

'She has no plans that I'm aware of. All I know is that Rory is keeping company with his father and some friends. It might be an old boys' kind of thing as Alex isn't invited.'

'Alex?'

'That's Rory's sister,' Morag answered. 'She's already met Sarah.'

'I see. So, what time should we meet tomorrow?'

'Lizzie has suggested I arrive at quarter to eleven. Coffee will be served at eleven o'clock.'

'She hasn't changed, then.' Cathy felt another twinge of panic. 'You obviously haven't told her who you're bringing.'

'Would you have?'

'No.'

'I'll come to the hotel tomorrow at ten so we can plan our campaign, if you like.'

'I'll be ready. Does she still disapprove of women wearing trousers?'

Morag snorted.

'I've no idea. But I reckon that is the least of our worries.'

★   ★   ★

Cathy chose to wear a navy blue shirt-dress with simple jewellery and

231

navy sandals. She was waiting in the foyer when Morag, wearing a trouser suit and blouse, pushed through the revolving door.

'How many years has it been since I gave you that farewell hug?' Cathy laughed as they fell upon each other and she realised neither of them were dry-eyed.

'Too many,' Morag said. 'I missed you dreadfully after you left. Going to a ceilidh was never the same without you to giggle with.' She looked around. 'I haven't been inside this place for years, but the manager sometimes calls at the café.'

'Mr Murray met me off the train. I was impressed.'

'A wee bird tells me he's impressed with Sarah.' Morag rolled her eyes. 'No doubt she'll explain everything when you see her.'

'I hope I haven't made a dreadful mistake, coming back here to rake up the past.'

'Nonsense! You're here for a purpose.

You have to defend your granddaughter and help the course of true love.'

'But it's such a short acquaintance between her and this young man.'

Morag's expression was quizzical.

'Don't you trust your granddaughter to know her own mind?'

Cathy nodded.

'All right, I deserved that.'

'It took you a while to find your soulmate. But you didn't go home and cut yourself off from life. You met someone and married him a few years later. You can hold your head up high. Now, let me tell you how I think we should play our cards . . . '

* * *

When Morag pulled up in the driveway of Rowan House, Cathy felt she understood what people meant by speaking of their heart being in their mouth.

She turned to her friend.

'What if Lizzie's housekeeper answers

the door and thinks I'm selling something?'

'We've been through this. You stand your ground and insist you have an appointment with Mrs McLean.'

Cathy sighed.

'I feel like it's my first day at school and I'm afraid to enter the classroom.'

'So you've come all this way just to sit in my car and let me go instead?'

'I'm sorry, Morag,' Cathy said. 'I'll do what I came to do, but please don't go too far, in case . . . '

Morag got out of the car and waited for Cathy to do the same.

'I'll walk slowly along the road and sit on that bench we passed. If you get thrown out, you can come and find me, though I'm hoping I can read a good chunk of my book before I see you next.' She winked at Cathy. 'Good luck, my dear.'

'Thanks, I'm going to need it.'

21

Look to the Future

Cathy approached the front entrance, noting the elaborate brass doorknocker gleamed as it always used to. The shrubs in the front garden were well tended and her feet trod on gravel that must have been freshly raked that morning.

Before she knew it she'd lifted the knocker and rapped twice, then twice again. It was as if the years had rolled back.

A quick glance at her watch reassured her the time was 10.45.

Cathy hardly had time to gather her wits before the door opened and a silver-haired woman, dressed in what looked like grey cashmere, stood before her, leaning on a silver-handled cane. Cathy took a deep, shuddery breath.

'Hello, Lizzie. It's been a long time.'

Lizzie McLean frowned.

'Do you know, when I heard that knock, I thought of you straightaway. No-one else taps like that.' She peered behind her visitor. 'Where's Morag?'

'Keeping out of the way.'

'And whose idea was this? Rory's?'

Cathy, suddenly feeling much braver, smiled.

'It was Morag who told me the relationship between my granddaughter and your grandson was developing, but visiting you is something I've thought about on and off for many years.'

'Then you'd better come in. The coffee's brewing.'

Cathy closed the heavy door behind her and looked around.

'Thank you for not sending me away, Lizzie. Should I fetch the tray?'

'My housekeeper's gone to the shops, so unless you prefer to sit in the kitchen, yes. This is one of my better days, but I don't think I can carry the coffee with one hand.'

Cathy hid a smile. Elizabeth McLean definitely hadn't changed.

In the sitting room there were colourful cushions and photographs, presumably of grandchildren, but the furniture looked just the same. On the wall above the fireplace, a wedding day portrait of Lizzie and James stared down at her. Now Cathy could look at it across the years and feel glad their marriage had been a happy one.

'Shall I pour?'

'Yes. Not too much milk for me, thank you.'

'I remember.' Cathy took Lizzie her cup and placed it on the table beside her.

'Come and sit on the settee so I don't have to strain to hear you.'

'You look very well, Lizzie.' Cathy settled herself.

Lizzie McLean shrugged.

'I can't complain. What about you, Cathy? You're still slim. Are you still married?'

'Widowed for three years now. He

was a lovely man.'

'Then we were both fortunate.'

The mantelpiece carriage clock ticked away while Cathy wondered how to begin.

'Just tell me what brings you here,' Lizzie said. 'Am I supposed to throw my arms around you and tell you all is forgiven?'

'I wouldn't expect that, Lizzie. It was Morag who told me I should come, but firstly I want to apologise for not explaining my feelings to you before I left Kirlaig.'

The older woman looked thoughtful.

'I wonder how I would have reacted if you had.'

'I didn't want to leave, but how could I possibly stay? I concocted a story about being urgently needed at home and my boss was very understanding. I hated lying, but I didn't think there was any other option.'

'And now, all these years later, it seems I'm the villain of the piece.' Lizzie leaned forward in her chair.

Cathy shook her head.

'Of course you're not. It must have been a dreadful shock to learn Sarah was in Kirlaig, bringing back memories you'd prefer remained buried. I've always believed that was a difficult time for James. If you'll forgive me for saying so, I think he needed a shoulder to cry on.'

She looked anxiously at her hostess. Time had etched plenty of lines on the older woman's face, but her eyes showed how alert she still was.

Lizzie nodded.

'It was a taxing time. I was edgy, anxious to have a bairn on the way, and James was working all the hours under the sun and having to tread on eggshells at home.' She reached for a handkerchief.

Cathy could stand it no longer. She rose and stood in front of Lizzie, stooping to put her arms around her.

'All three of us found true happiness in the end. Lizzie, please, how can it be right to deny the same privilege to Rory and Sarah?'

*   *   *

Sarah was in the café kitchen, stirring a pan of vegetable soup and feeling proud about making it from scratch, when her mobile phone began ringing. She put down the wooden spoon and reached into her pocket, frowning when she saw the caller's identity.

'Gran, is everything all right?'

'Very much so, darling. Guess where I am?'

Sarah began stirring again. She knew her gran was trying to revisit all the museums she'd been taken to as a child.

'The Museum Of London? I know it's on your list.'

'I'm at Rowan House with Lizzie and Morag.' Cathy sounded triumphant.

'Gran, can you say that again? I must have misheard.'

'You didn't mishear, Sarah. As I

speak, Lizzie is sitting in the hall, talking to young Rory, as she calls him, on the phone.'

Sarah felt breathless. She put down the spoon again.

'But when did you get here? Does this mean what I think it means?'

'I arrived last night. That nice Alistair Murray met me off the train. Everything's happened in a rush but I'm so thrilled to be here. Morag's bringing me to the café in a while. Lizzie's been making phone calls and we're all invited to a meal this evening.'

Sarah's eyes filled with tears.

'I can't believe it. Rory's gran has relented? She really wants to meet me?'

'Cross my heart and hope to die! I'll see you soon, darling.'

Sarah ended the call and checked the soup of the day was simmering nicely. She'd hardly put her phone away, trying to take this startling news on board, and wondering whether to try Rory's number, when her mobile rang again.

'It's me.' It was Rory.

'Thank goodness. I think I'm about to have a fit of the vapours.'

'Try not to. I don't think that particular condition's one of my specialities.'

She laughed.

'Alistair told me he was meeting someone from London off the train. Who'd have thought my gran would have the bottle to come all this way?'

'Who'd have thought mine could change her tune so quickly?'

'I wish I could see you, Rory,' Sarah told him.

'Same here. But I'm carrying out home visits and holding a clinic this afternoon. Soraiya's on holiday this week.'

'I understand. Should I offer to help your grandmother, or is that a bit pushy?'

'Not at all, but she's asked my sister to cook and I'm sure Alex will appreciate some help later. I make a good butler!'

'I can't wait. But I'm beginning to feel nervous.'

'I know it's been a difficult time but that's over now,' Rory assured her. 'You've no need to be nervous. Just be yourself and from now on we can plan our future.'

'I'm as relieved as you are, Rory, but I'd just like to say, Soraiya told me about your welcome home party. Were you going to tell me about it?'

'I'm sorry I didn't say anything to you. I made it clear to Nana that I wouldn't be attending unless she was prepared to invite you. You might be pleased to hear that when she rang me just now, she apologised for any hurt she's caused us. I've told her I think it's high time for us all to forget the past and look to the future.'

★   ★   ★

By the time the day of Rory's party arrived, Sarah's grandma had moved into Rowan House, at Lizzie McLean's request. Rory's family had all wanted her to stay on so she could

243

attend the celebration.

'It's weird but I feel as though I've been back for months already,' Rory told Sarah while they were arranging chairs round the oak dining table on the Saturday afternoon.

'Well, it's six weeks and four days since we met.'

'Why is it women always remember these things?' Smiling, he walked round to her side of the table and took her in his arms.

She snuggled against him.

'Happy?' he asked.

'What do you think?'

'So, is it too soon to ask you a very important question?'

'Yes,' she said sternly. 'If it's what I suspect it is. Do you really want to upset your grandmother again?'

He kissed the tip of her nose.

'She's really not the strict matriarch she likes everyone to think she is.'

'I know, and she's been very welcoming to me. Gran's thrilled to bits, and as for Morag, when those three get together it's priceless to hear them.'

'And it's all down to you, Sarah Barnes.' He tipped her chin upwards and kissed her on the lips this time.

'It's all down to Morag, you mean,' she said moments later. 'She even apologised for all the fibs she had to tell me!'

'All in a good cause,' he said.

'I'm a bit nervous about meeting your mother and all the other new people,' Sarah admitted.

'Well, Ma only got home last night, but she says she's very much looking forward to meeting you. You've already met Pa. And Alex's boyfriend's a good guy.' He grinned. 'You can talk to Fiona about how terrible it is being my girlfriend, and I went to school with Andy. It'll be good to catch up again.'

'I can't wait for you to meet my folks,' Sarah said.

'If your mum takes after Cathy, we should get on well. Have you told your parents yet? About us, I mean.'

'I might have.' She laughed. 'Of

course I have, but they're still travelling and the line wasn't great. They're due back soon, but it's unlikely I'll make it home until the end of the summer.'

She watched his expression.

'My new job will end after September, Rory, when there aren't so many tourists about.'

'I thought you said Morag had invited you to stay whenever you wanted.'

'She has, but if I want to continue with what I trained for, I've no hope of doing so around here.'

He nodded.

'You were insistent I shouldn't throw everything up and join a practice in London. Now it's my turn. If I'm staying in Kirlaig, we both know the only way we can be together is for you to remain, too.'

She nodded.

'Of course.'

He glanced at the clock.

'We have so much to talk about and so many decisions to make, but we need to get this party over with first. When the time comes, I can take a few days off and accompany you to London.'

She flung herself into his arms again.

'That's perfect, Rory. We'd have loads of time to talk on the train! Unlike last time,' she added slyly.

He hugged her to him.

'We may not have known each other for long, but we've had enough ups and downs to last us a while, don't you think?'

'It's worth it, though.'

He hugged her again.

'You bet. Now it's time to go back and get changed. I'll drop you off at Morag's and pick you both up at seven.'

'It's a good job I packed that little black dress!' she said.

⋆　⋆　⋆

Sarah gazed around the dining room. She was seated next to Rory, with Fiona's boyfriend, Andy, on the other side. Her grandmother, wearing a black

247

lace dress, sat opposite, with Rory's father and Lizzie on one side and his mum and Morag on the other. Alex and her boyfriend Jack were opposite Fiona and Andy. The remaining couple was Soraiya McGregor and her husband.

Rory leaned into Sarah.

'I told you everything would be fine. Mind you, a couple of weeks ago I wasn't too sure how things would work out.'

'We mustn't look backwards,' Sarah said. 'My goodness, these look wonderful!'

She gazed at the desserts arranged on the plate in front of her.

'A miniature cream meringue, a tiny raspberry tart and something dark and deliciously chocolatey.'

'I'm not sure the doctor would order that,' Rory said, straight-faced. 'But tonight's a special occasion.'

'Very special,' she agreed.

'I've been thinking hard most of the day. About your future, Sarah.'

'Oh?' She raised her eyebrows.

'I think you'd make a fantastic teacher. Would you ever consider retraining?'

She chased a raspberry round her plate.

'Great minds think alike. I've been researching courses at Fort Robert.'

'The University of the Western Highlands.' Rory's eyes sparkled as he looked at her. 'It's not too far away to travel and there would be days when you could work from home.'

'There aren't that many high schools in the area, but I could enquire about teaching in further education.'

Rory nodded.

'You already have an excellent degree. All this sounds very positive,' he replied.

'I didn't want you to feel I wasn't one hundred percent behind you. After all, if I'm to be a doctor's wife one day, I'll need some special qualities.' Sarah sneaked a sideways glance at Rory. 'Well, what do you think, Doctor?'

'I . . . I think I feel a proposal coming on. Now tell me it's far too soon to become engaged — if you dare!' He put down his spoon, pushed his chair away from the table and got down on one knee.

Conversation faded away as everyone focused their attention on Rory.

'Sarah, will you do me the honour of becoming my wife?'

She was afraid to meet anyone's gaze. No-one said a word. But the surge of happiness she felt was unmistakable.

'I will. Oh, yes, please, Rory!'

He stood up again and she was in his arms.

Rory's mother, father and sister were on their feet, ready to congratulate the young couple. Soraiya, dazzling in a magenta silk gown, signalled her delight with a loud 'Woohoo' across the table.

But there was only one person whose approval Sarah sought. Rory's grandma reached out her arms and embraced her

'I couldn't be more delighted,' Lizzie said. 'The McLean men always have excellent taste when it comes to choosing a wife.'